McGowan's Retreat

Also by Rob Smith:

McGowan's Call (fiction)
Night Voices (fiction)
Hogwarts, Narnia, and Middle Earth (criticism)
256 Zones of Gray (poetry)

McGowan's Retreat

Rob Smith

Drinian Press/
Huron, Ohio

Cover design and photograph © Drinian Press

Drinian Press, LLC
P.O. Box 63
Huron, Ohio 44839
Visit our Web site at: www.DrinianPress.com

Library of Congress Control Number: 2009902709

(Hardcover)
ISBN-10: 0-9820609-3-9
ISBN-13: 978-0-9820609-3-3

(Paperback)
ISBN-10: 0-9820609-4-7
ISBN-13: 978-0-9820609-4-0

Printed in the United States of America

For Nancy

Chapter One

Bendy Ditch

For most of the year, the Bendy Ditch gurgles quietly and doesn't carry enough water to officially make Elkhorn, South Dakota a backwater settlement. It does, however, lend its name to almost every business in the small town. Though difficult to find, Davis McGowan was on a mission, and he had managed to locate the elusive settlement of Elkhorn. It was marked on a road map that he bought at a busy truck stop just west of Sioux Falls.

"Here it is," he said to his wife. Beth was taking her turn at the wheel on the long drive between Dayton, Ohio and Bozeman, Montana.

"Don't tell me that you've found the Garden of Eden?" she queried with a soft laugh.

"Better that that," said Davis, "I have actually found Elkhorn, South Dakota which lies at the very crossroads of paradise. No, I take that back; Elkhorn doesn't appear to be a crossroads to anywhere at all. There's one road that goes in, and it just stops. The map doesn't actually name the famous Bendy Ditch, but there is a twisty blue line that runs east into another line that's marked 'Oak,' which must be a river or creek."

"So the place really exists?" added Beth.

"Apparently it does, and it is just where Shelly said it would be. If we get off I-90 at Presho, we'll be, maybe, fifteen miles from checking out her story. I'm telling you that it doesn't look like much on this map."

When Davis found the small dot of a town, they were driving past an exit for Montrose, and Presho was still over an hour away (maybe an hour-and-a-half if the speed limit signs meant anything). Even before they found it on the map, they had resolved to make the out-of-the-way trek if only to test the reality of a tale that seemed farfetched.

Their friend, Shelly Martin, had been the pastor of the Elkhorn Methodist Church for eleven years. Towards the end of that time she married Jerry Ferguson, a Presbyterian minister in Miller. This was a second marriage for both. They had each lost their spouses through long illnesses.

Both having recently lost a spouse, it only seemed natural that the Methodist pastor at Miller would introduce Jerry to Shelly. Despite the geographical awkwardness of their dating relationship, their cautious courtship outlasted the paralysis of their individual grief. They secretly dated well-away from their home turf, and met often for dinner at a restaurant in Pierre. When each announced their engagement to their respective congregations, everyone was taken by surprise. Everyone, that is, except the minister friend who had introduced them. The Rev. Jack Warren enjoyed the coup that the three had pulled. "Imagine," he said, "three pastors from small towns knowing something before the grapevine has a chance to invent its own retelling of the story."

Initially, the reaction to the wedding was good all 'round, and everyone was happy that the two had found companionship in each other. But then reality began to wrap its ugly fingers around a hundred-and-fifty miles of blacktop. Where would the couple live?

Both congregations had the same simple, obvious answer. They each loved and respected their leader, and each knew that the other parish would completely understand when the newlyweds would come to live in their town. Of course, that argument became a brutal tug-of-war that was thinly disguised as affection. The other fact that was obvious was that living midway in Pierre was out of the question on both sides. Only Shelly and Jerry could see the benefit of living *in-between* with cell phones to keep all the telephone calls local.

The most surprising option came from some of the members at Elkhorn. Dinner reservations were made for the couple in a private dining room of the Bendy Ditch Hotel. While Jerry was still trying to decide between the Maine lobster (which he was assured was fresh), and the Angus beef (which he knew to be local), their host offered a wedding present.

"The community of Elkhorn, as you may now suspect," began Dennis Jensen, "has many more resources than you might guess in a town of our size. We have prepared an offer. Jerry, if you choose to settle in Elkhorn, we could eliminate the need for either of you to commute. Right now we are willing to replace your current salary and you could work here alongside Shelly."

"But you don't even know what I make," he protested, "and I'm sure the District Superintendent would have something to say about adding a Presbyterian to the staff of a small church."

"Well, as far as that goes," Jensen continued, "the District Superintendent and the Bishop understand us, and we know quite well what you currently make. Frankly, we don't want to insult the people of Miller by offering you too much more, but we could do that. Come up with a number: I'm sure we can work something out."

"No, no, that's fine."

"One more thing, there's also a condo in Hilton Head which is yours for the week after Easter each year. We saw what Shelly went through when her husband was so sick. This will be our way of giving you both an early break from the Dakota winter and, at the same time, give you newlyweds some time alone."

Even Shelly, who knew better the ways of Elkhorn, had not been prepared for an offer like this. Jensen suddenly closed his menu, set aside his white linen napkin, and stood up from the table. "You both have a lot to talk about. Take your time, and enjoy your dinner." With that he left the room; Jerry and Shelly sat as mirror images of dropped jaws.

** ** **

"Maybe it is the Garden of Eden," said Davis, coming back to reality.

They saw Elkhorn like a red brick wall rising out of the rolling prairie grasses. Its one main street formed a canyon which funneled the road into the rift between the terra cotta pillars that was the gateway to the town. Visible behind the line of shops were modest white-framed houses, though there were no apparent roads leading back toward them. The entrance to the residential areas was either at the far end of town or through the several narrow alleys that cut between the store fronts.

By now, Beth had slowed the car to a crawl. The single avenue looked like a colorized photo from the early twentieth century. Black wrought iron street lamps and green awnings broke the square lines of the one and two-storied buildings. On the taller buildings, windows framed in white sandstone looked down on the boulevard. In Hatteras, Ohio where Beth and Davis had lived for nearly a decade, there were similar buildings, but they were punctuated by neglect and boarded-up storefronts. These buildings looked fresh enough to be a modern recreation meant to mimic the days when prosperous towns sprouted out of the prairie following along the course of the railroads.

"Wow!" said Beth. "There's a lot of money here."

"But where does it come from?" asked Davis. "I can't see how these places could stay in business without customers. How many people live here?"

"Can't be that many, there are only a couple dozen houses."

As Shelly had told them, the storefronts nearly all bore the same generic name. On just one side of the road, there were the Bendy Ditch Café, the Bendy Ditch Cinema, the Bendy Ditch Market, and the Bendy Ditch Cable Company. The only enterprise that appeared to have a national franchise was the Elkhorn Methodist Church, which sat all by itself at the end of town and wore the denominational flaming vermilion scarf of its logo on the welcoming sign.

"There's Shelly's old church," observed Beth.

The road ended at a single stop sign. Straight ahead was a natural, unbroken western panorama of the South Dakota grasslands. A right turn led into a gated community that bore the title "Bendy Ditch Estates". Davis' best guess was that there were about twenty-five upscale homes in the neighborhood. In Dayton, Ohio, the least of these houses would run five hundred thousand dollars even after the housing bubble broke in 2008. "Wow is right!" he added. "It's too rich for us."

Even more out-of-place, however, was the building on the left. A quarter mile from where they sat was a long, three-storied gray stone building. It sat low enough in the rolling landscape to be invisible from the entrance to town, but here it commanded the view. The manicured lawn of the surrounding grounds looked like a lush carpet of green. Davis immediately thought of Nassau Hall at Princeton University. But what was a Georgian-Colonial building doing here with its massive white cupola shining in the early summer sun of the Dakotas? A landscape engineer had marked the access route with a formal sign reading "Elkhorn Management Institute". A subtitle floated beneath on invisible supports, "Architects of Free Enterprise".

"There's the money," offered Beth. Since gates blocked the roads left and right, it was obvious that the road went no further for the uninitiated. Beth made a U-turn and headed the car back toward town.

"Seen enough?" Davis asked, "Or do we go for the deluxe treatment?" In this case the *deluxe treatment* was Shelly's suggestion that if they were unconvinced about her claims for Elkhorn, they should take a room for the night at the hotel.

"I say that we go for it!"

"You mean that you're not convinced?" he asked.

"No, I am now a true believer. But, I also know that we have a four-person tent in the trunk and right now this adventure seems better than an air mattress in a state park!"

** ** **

It was only a very short distance back to the town, but this time Davis and Beth kept their eyes open for clues about parking. It was as they suspected. The paved cutouts between clusters of buildings, though no larger than alleyways, led to off-street parking lots behind the shops. The odd thing was the lack of signage. Like most small towns, these passages were set up for the locals. Only tourists need directions; evidently, Elkhorn was not set up for visitors.

"I'll bet there aren't many secrets in this place," offered Davis.

"And we were spotted the moment we pulled in," said Beth. "I wished we'd dressed up a bit." She was now noticing the few people who were walking along the main street. The McGowans had worn jeans and light sweaters; here the people were more *corporate casual.*

"Explains about Jerry and Shelly, doesn't it?"

"Sure does," agreed Beth.

While there was no doubt that Jerry Ferguson and Shelly Martin were a devoted couple, they had very different views of attire. Shelly looked corporate, always. Since moving to Ohio, Jerry had cut back on his western style, but still wore a silver belt buckle with the words "Cowboy Up" emblazoned on the polished face.

"Did I ever tell you what Jerry said when I asked him about his belt buckle?" Davis chuckled with his memory.

"No, at least I don't remember you saying anything."

"He said he like the sentiment behind 'Cowboy Up' and he couldn't figure out an Ohio-Midwestern equivalent other than 'Suck it up, Whiny,' but that wouldn't fit on the buckle."

"Yep, that sounds like Jerry," said Beth. "Of course, we women are more gifted with personal expressions. We would say, 'Put on your big-girl panties and deal with it!'"

"Don't tell that to Jerry, he might just do it. 'Cowboy Up' is fine!"

** ** **

Neither Beth nor Davis were prepared for what they found when they crossed over the threshold of the Bendy Ditch Hotel. The exterior simply looked like a modest two-story brick building with storefront windows set up to look like a small gift shop. Inside, however, the space opened up to high ceilings and deep carpet. The desk staff, male and female, wore neat navy blazers and focused on computer screens built into the polished oak counters. At the end of the counter a brass sign identified the concierge.

"Wow," said Davis. "You're right; I wish we'd dressed for the occasion."

"May I help you, sir?" said a pleasant voice. Davis turned to face a well-groomed young man with two bars on the cuff of his sleeve. Davis took them to be some sort of insignia of rank.

"Do you have any rooms available?" asked

Davis.

"Are you with the Institute?" asked the young man.

"No," said McGowan. "We are just in town for a short visit."

"And how many nights are you planning to stay?"

"Just one. Actually, we're here because we've heard so much about the town from a friend who used to live here."

The young man's features softened with the hint of a smile. "It's a very small town. Who is your friend?"

"Shelly Martin," said Davis. "She was the minister at the Methodist Church for a number of years."

"Of course," said the man. "Everybody knew Reverend Shelly. I'll tell you what. The Institute has blocked out all of our rooms for a conference they are hosting, but we won't know until one o'clock whether they will need them all. If you would like to leave your name with me, you could get a bite of lunch, and come back in an hour or so... I should know by then if one is available for the night."

Davis jotted his name on a small notepad that the young man had slid across the counter to him. In an effort to upgrade their appearance, he wrote "Dr. and Mrs. Davis McGowan."

"Thank you, Dr. McGowan," said the man politely.

As an afterthought Davis asked, "What are your regular room rates?"

"Standard rate for a double begins at two hundred and fifty dollars a night, but we offer discounts for automobile clubs and the like."

McGowan tried to not swallow too hard, and calmly followed up with, "Where do you recommend that we eat?"

"There are really only two places in town," said the man with practiced clarity. "The hotel has a restaurant and there's the Bendy Ditch Café that you must have driven by when you entered town."

"We've heard about the hotel, so maybe we'll try it first."

"Very good, Sir. Check back in about an hour, and I should have an answer for you."

Beth and Davis set off in the direction that he had indicated. They found themselves in an alley of shops. What appeared as small individual shops from the outside street were actually a small indoor mall offering jewelry and gifts as well as a barber shop and beauty salon. They waited for the hostess who, as the McGowans noticed, seated them away from the center of the room and out of sight of most of the diners.

Surprisingly, the dining room did a brisk lunch trade. The male patrons sported ties, the women, tailored suits. When they were settled in the booth, Beth was the first to notice that the least expensive item on the menu was a burger at $14.95, extra if you wanted cheese.

"Are we in Chicago?" she asked.

"Sure feels that way," said Davis. "When Shelly began these stories about the small town paradise, she forgot to mention the cost of living!"

"Oh well," sighed Beth, "it's our vacation splurge and we can just put it on plastic and deal with it later."

"I don't think that this is really a small town," said Davis. "It is exactly as Shelly told us; it's a laboratory for the Institute. They need model businesses to own and manage and, in exchange, the locals get full employment and big city amenities in small town America."

"Along with big city prices," added Beth.

** ** **

After the initial price shock, lunch proved enjoyable. The food was presented with care, and the server, a middle-aged woman named Becky, seemed genuinely friendly and paid attention to her tables. Instead of an endless repetition of "Is everything okay, here?" she timed her visits to coincide with the ebb and flow of the McGowans' conversation.

For Beth and Davis, it felt like the beginning of a long-needed respite. Davis had just completed his first year as an Instructor at Wright State University. He had elected to take early retirement from parish ministry to become both the oldest and most junior member of the Departments of Religion and Philosophy. After the pressures of congregational life, the University offered an opportunity to pursue his love of teaching without the pastoral burdens. For the most part, students were young, and, though they faced the dread of finals, they were not usually facing the imminent loss of life. For the instructor there was the downside of another sort of pressure. It was the plodding through less than stirring term papers, tabulating some sort of class participation grade, and bundling exam scores to make some plausible tally of achievement. But grades had been turned in a week ago, and the surge of student complaints had subsided. Today he was in Elkhorn, South Dakota having a leisurely lunch with Beth. The price of that meal seemed inconsequential to the moment.

It was already past one o'clock when they noticed the time. After settling with Becky, they took an unhurried stroll back to the front desk of the hotel. Beth looked at a designer scarf in one of the boutiques, then changed her mind when she looked at the tag. The young desk clerk addressed them as they approached.

"Dr. McGowan," he began, "I'm sorry, but there's been a bit of a snag. The Institute not only requires all the rooms that they had reserved, we are scrambling to see if we can free up a few more."

"Their business must be brisk," said Davis.

Ignoring him, the clerk continued. "I would be glad to confirm reservations for you and Mrs. McGowan at another hotel. There are some fine accommodations both east and west along Interstate 90."

"Oh, that's not necessary," said Davis. "We just might try to put some miles behind us tonight. We're headed to Bozeman to see our son." The excuse sounded plausible enough. The truth was that in light of the opulence of the hotel, he had not wanted to admit that the fallback position for the night was a tent in the Badlands.

"Very well, sir. I hope you have a pleasant visit." McGowan turned to leave, then, as an afterthought, turned back to the clerk.

"Would you like me to give your regards to Shelly Martin?"

The man's expression dimmed. "I believe I misspoke earlier. When you said 'Shelly' I was thinking of Sheldon Marvin who worked at the cable company. We used to call him Shelly, too. Sorry."

"No problem. Mistakes happen." Davis and Beth

headed toward the door. Neither spoke until they were outside in the bright midday sun.

"What happened in there?" asked Beth.

"I think," said Davis, "that we were just run out of town!"

Chapter Two

On the Run

The trip to Montana turned out to be the first of many in a getaway season for the McGowans. They were only at their house in Fairborn long enough to pay the bills and mow the grass which had grown so long that it choked the mower every six or eight feet. In the end, he and Beth had created a mountain of clippings for the compost pile.

Among the messages on their answering machine was one from the Presbytery office regarding a new volunteer assignment. Since his retirement, Davis had stepped back from most of his involvement in the denomination. It was not that he was opposed to what was going on so much as the fact that life as a college professor took place in a parallel universe and made him feel out of step in the world of parish life. Campus life was very clearly focused into blocks of time and subject matter. The ministry, on the other hand, always took twists and turns. You could awaken in the morning with a clear schedule of how the day was to unfold, and one phone call would erase it all. All the jokes about ministers working one day a week were tiring. People assumed that sermon preparation was the most time consuming part of the work week. In reality, that was a task that could be adlibbed at the last moment in a way that a funeral or hospital visit could not. During his days in the parish, summer was a time for laying out the church year with everything that was predictable like Christmas, Easter, teacher recognition, and topics for the adult class. Once September rolled around and the schedule took off there would be little time for creative thinking. Just do everything that is pressing and stick to the game-plan for everything else. That was his mantra. The summer-made plans were the closest thing to having autopilot when time itself got out of control.

At the University, the Department provided a schedule, and he needed only to tweak a syllabus and figure out how to motivate students into learning when their first priority was getting a grade and a credit toward graduation. "My job," he would tell them, "is to get inside your head and mess you up forever!"

In this particular regard, it was a lot like church ministry. Congregations, for the most part, are mixed bags. They include people from all backgrounds and walks of life. Their political views are left, right, and center and a handful of them always think that it is their personal mission to make sure that whatever comes from the pulpit fits their preference, whether left, right, or center. McGowan always tried to hold his politics close and figured, as a pastor, it was his job to keep the people together around a view of shared values rather than a homogenized pattern of words. Some members understood, but students were much easier to deal with in the sense that they knew some of whatever he said might show up on an exam.

When he called the Presbytery Executive, the old frustrations started to churn in his stomach. He was relieved when the "assignment" turned out to be unproblematic. Shelly Martin was beginning the process of transferring her credentials from the Methodist Church to the Presbyterian. The two denominations worked closely together, and the bureaucratic red tape wasn't all that sticky. Transcripts and references would have to be checked, but, as Davis knew, Shelly was a Garrett Seminary graduate, and credentials would not be a great barrier. In any case, that sort of checking would all be done via committee. What the Executive wanted was to recruit Davis as a mentor for Shelly during her transitional year. As if Davis needed an extra nudge, "Jerry and Shelly specifically requested that you be asked," was added. The endorsement was unneces-

25

sary. Though Beth and Davis had only recently met Jerry and Shelly, it was obvious that the two couples had a great deal in common. Conversation between them was quick and easy, and the visit to Elkhorn seemed only reasonable in light of the McGowans' commitment to a developing friendship. Shelly's request for Davis as a mentor proved the feelings were reciprocated.

"I'd be glad to," was Davis' reply. He had thought of adding, "Of course they asked for me, it'll be fun," but thought better of it. "I'll set up a preliminary meeting today," was his actual reply.

He hung up the phone and rummaged through the desk drawer that caught all the important mail. He found what he was looking for, the brochure announcing the fall program for the Dayton Philharmonic.

"Beth, what do you think about asking Jerry and Shelly to join us for the first orchestra concert of the season?"

"What's that?" asked his wife from the other room.

"I was just asked to be a mentor for Shelly Martin, and I figured that it might be fun for the four of us to go to the Schuster Center for a concert," he called back.

"Sure," she said, "and we can tease her about highfalutin Elkhorn."

"You may," said Davis, "but I will have to restrain myself. After all, I am her mentor and will have to be gracious and hospitable."

"Right!"

** ** **

The phone call to Shelly and Jerry was brief, but welcomed. Shelly was glad to have a personal friend as a mentor, and even happier with the prospect of a night out with the McGowans. Davis and Beth already had season tickets for the classical concert series, but agreed to pick up an extra pair for the September performance. They might not have seats together, but would try get something in the same section.

In turn, Ferguson had suggested dinner before the concert, and they agreed on the gourmet pizza bistro at Town and Country Shopping Center in Kettering. Davis started to say, "Where the Peasant Stock Restaurant used to be," but he stopped himself. That was small town insider-talk. As far as Martin and Ferguson knew, the place had always served pizza.

By seven o'clock the next morning, Beth and Davis were already on the road and heading north to spend the last weeks of summer sailing the Lake Erie Islands. Their sailboat was docked at Harbor

North on the Huron River, and they would be loading groceries into the galley within three hours. While the trip to Montana had shown them the waves of grain, they were now ready to feel the rhythm of water against the hull of their sailing sloop.

Chapter Three

===

Scudder to South Bass

The route between Dayton and Huron was well-traveled by the McGowans. It took them across many small towns and open farm country. They knew every fast food restaurant and rest stop along the way, and which had the cleanest rest rooms. As they approached Huron from the west, Beth said, "I wish that we had remembered to get a book that we could read aloud while we're sailing."

The two had listened to audio books on the long drive to Montana, but those had been returned to the library during their brief stay at the house. They would not do much good in any case since there was no CD player on the boat. Today, they wanted to get going as quickly as possible. Their goal was to get to Scudder on the north end of Pelee Island in Ontario. With the wind steady and from the west, the trip would take about ten hours. Without a steady wind, the same ten hours would be accompanied by the noise and smell of the old diesel engine. Beth and Davis had already decided that, in the event of wind failure, they'd head, instead, for Put-in-Bay on South Bass Island. That destination would only be six hours away, and they could make for Scudder on the following day. The trick was to get going before the afternoon heat created the dreaded doldrums of windless water.

The trunk of the car held all the provisions except for a half gallon of milk which they picked up at the mini-market on the corner just down from the marina. Within a half-hour the store of supplies was aboard, and Davis was on the foredeck hanking on the foresail. Beth made a last trip to the washroom and returned to the boat wearing a broad smile borrowed from the proverbial cat.

"What did you do?" asked Davis.

"I bought a book to read," she said.

"From the marina office?" queried Davis. "Is it one of the used books that gets shared around?"

"No, this one is new. It's written by an author that lives here in town."

"Like that's going to be any good," said McGowan cynically.

"Don't jump to conclusions, it can't be all bad. It even has some of the things you like in it."

"Like what?"

"Like sailing and anthropology. They also pointed out that if you look very closely at the back cover you can see the roller coasters at Cedar Point."

She held up the book which pictured an ice-covered break wall and an expanse of open water. Davis took it from her hand and flipped it over. The panorama on the back cover showed a hazy coastline. Beth was right. If you looked carefully, through the haze was the Roller Coaster Capital of the World!

"Okay," he said laughing. "I'll give it one chapter!"

"That's why I love you," she said, "you're so open-minded."

** ** **

As the day unfolded, it was showing more and more promise. A new front was advancing with rank on rank of cloud formations, and with the clouds came the wind. Beth and Davis set their course by the compass and headed toward magnetic north. It was nearly a straight line that would take them over the horizon and out of sight of all land for a brief period of time. When terra firma reappeared, they would be in Canadian waters and moving on a heading parallel with the eastern shore of Pelee Island. The only potential obstacle on this passage would be the commercial fishing nets, and Davis would have to keep his eyes peeled to avoid the long lines of floating markers that would block their forward progress. Nets were always a challenge and sailing around and between the lines of floats was like walking a maze.

The sails had already been hoisted before they reached the mouth of the river, and they sailed out into the lake past the light that marked the entrance to the lake. Huron is in the southernmost basin of Lake Erie, the wide bay that gives Ohio its distinctive heart shape. To the east is a water tower that marks the City of Vermilion. Behind them now was the plume of white smoke from the lime plant standing on the river's eastern bank. To the west, in the haze, are the arching rails of the roller coasters of Cedar Point Amusement Park. Even from that distance, the sliding cars rolled quickly downhill only to creep up the next ridge of the steel rails.

"I think that when people get to the very top of those coasters, they can look out on the lake and see the sails on the water," said Davis, "and then, they wish they were on the boat instead of that lunch loser!"

"Speaking of roller coasters," began Beth, "we have a new book."

"Okay, but just one chapter!" protested Davis.

Beth pulled out the copy of *Night Voices* and began to read. It was as advertised, and when she offered to go below and fix lunch, Davis suggested reading another chapter first.

They were both past ready to call it a day when

they rounded the northeast corner of Pelee. To the right and toward the Canadian mainland they could see the major channel for the Great Lakes shipping. On the left, the ruins of an old lighthouse marked the shallow waters close to the island. Straight ahead in the center of the island was the grain elevator that marked the small village of Scudder. As they approached the marina, Davis hailed the harbormaster on his handheld radio. They were given docking instructions and told which side of the boat they should place their fenders. When they arrived at their assigned dock, shore crew were at the ready to help with the dock lines. Scudder is a quiet retreat. At the marina office Davis paid for two nights' dockage and made the mandatory call to Canadian Customs. After reading off the boat's identifying numbers, the voice at the other end of the line said, "Welcome to Canada, Dr. McGowan. Is your wife, Beth, with you?"

"Yes, she is," he said.

"Do you have any other passengers aboard?"

"No, we are traveling alone." Davis was always impressed by the tone of hospitality from the representatives of Canada. Obviously, their politeness was undergirded with efficiency. He was in their national database and they knew the vessel and the names of its usual crew. After clarifying length of stay and that there were no firearms or volumes of liquor aboard, the visit was authorized.

"Enjoy your stay in Canada, Dr. McGowan." Davis knew that they would enjoy Pelee Island, not for its attractions, but for its lack of distractions. It was a quiet place with spectacular sunsets, brilliant starry nights, and breezes that came unobstructed over the water. That evening, Beth and Davis watched the sunset and slept in the forward cabin with the hatch open to the stars.

Between the winery and the small beach, the McGowans loved this little island where the main sights included cornfields and big sky. They spent the next day walking the dusty roads, and wading along the small beach that bordered on the marina.

The return trip to the States would provide a balance to the monastic quiet of a day on Pelee Island. The following morning, they cast off their dock lines and set out from the village of Scudder. As they motored out of the harbor, they passed the day-mark at the entrance to the break wall. Beth checked the wind indicator at the top of the mast. The wind was blowing from the north, straight over the bow.

Davis went up on deck to raise the sails. When he finished, it was time to point the boat west. They would sail around the island and then turn south toward Put-in-Bay, which was located on the southernmost of the three Bass Islands. With increased attention to homeland security, they fully expected to be boarded by the Coast Guard when they passed over the international border. While they did see the patrol boats, they were not boarded. On the other hand, they were following a direct line toward the narrow slot that ran between Middle and South Bass Islands. To a trained observer this was an indication that they were heading toward the village of Put-in-Bay which nestled against the shore of a natural harbor. Besides being a favorite destination for the party crowd, Put-in-Bay features a videophone where boaters from Canada can register with the U.S. authorities.

The Bay itself has a history. Soon after the out-break of war in 1812, the British took control of the waters of Lake Erie and captured Detroit. In 1813, Oliver Hazard Perry was put in charge of the American naval forces and took control of Presque Isle (now Erie, Pennsylvania). The British under Robert Heriot Barclay set up a blockade, but a sand-bar blocked his ships from a final assault on the young navy. Lack of provisions and bad weather forced Barclay to break off the siege. While they re-supplied, the Americans emptied their own boats and literally hauled them over the sand. Four days later, when Barclay returned, Perry had his smaller gunboats ready for action. The British backed off to wait for reinforcement.

Perry moved his boats to the west end of the lake

and took on additional recruits. In some ways, the tables had turned. Now the British were effectively bottled up in the western waters of Lake Erie. Perry's fleet set up an anchorage at Put-in-Bay near South Bass Island. As supplies dwindled, Barclay had little choice but to try and break the blockade by going on the attack. On September 10, 1813, word came to Perry that the British flotilla was coming to engage them in battle. When Perry's flagship, the *Lawrence*, came under fire, four-fifths of the crew were killed or wounded in the exchange. Perry, himself, was rowed half a mile to the *Niagara* after taking down his personal pennant, a blue flag with the motto: "Don't Give Up the Ship." He didn't. Barclay had expected that Perry and the *Niagara* would lead the American ships in retreat; instead Perry took to the offensive. In the end, Perry won the day and accepted the British surrender aboard the wreck of the *Lawrence*. Historians report that he did this so that Barclay could witness the human price paid for the victory. Of more lasting fame, however, is the handwritten message he sent to General William Henry Harrison, "We have met the enemy, and he is ours."

Today, Put-in-Bay remembers those times in names like Ballast Island and the Perry Victory Monument. At three hundred fifty-two feet tall, it is the world's most massive Doric column. To be politically correct, the monument has a second name, the International Peace Memorial. If it is a bit confusing to have a single monument dedicated to both war and peace, that subtlety is lost on the army of visitors who come to the Bay to shop and/or party on the little island that sometimes forgets to go to sleep at night during the summer months.

Beth and Davis furled the sails and motored into the harbor; the monument with its green lawn was on their left and the sheer rock-face of Gibraltar Island on the right. Ahead was the quaint town with rows of docks and the Boathouse Restaurant at the head of a row of waterfront businesses. Davis used his handheld radio to hail the dock master. Their intent was to tie off to one of the mooring buoys placed in the bay behind the protection of Gibraltar Island which sits on the northern edge of the Bay. It has all the markings of a small campus, and for good reason. Once the headquarters for Perry's campaign, it's now a research facility for Ohio State University. The dock that provides access to the private island sits directly in front of a rectangular brick building that gives it a collegiate look, and attests to its function as a research facility for studying the conditions of the Great Lakes.

Since it was not a weekend, there were many open spaces, and the dock master told them to choose a spot and settle in. They motored across the bay to put as much distance as they could between their anchorage and the Boathouse. Sound carries well over the water, so the idea of putting space between the boat and late-night revelers was an exercise in futility, but it was what Beth and Davis always did. After rigging a shade awning over the boom, Davis used his radio to call a water taxi. As they sat on deck, they saw the blue-hulled power launch put out from the Boathouse. There were eight passengers on board. It zigzagged its way through the maze of anchored boats pulling alongside hulls letting passengers off on some, picking up new riders from others. All day long the small boats ferry yachtsmen to shore and back.

When the neat launch came alongside the McGowans' boat, there were three others on board. They were also headed ashore. The McGowans stepped over to the taxi and took a seat on one of the polished teak benches. In a few minutes, the boat was pulling alongside the pier, and the passengers stepped up and out of the water taxi.

Davis paid the mooring fees and then disembarked. He and Beth had their passports and ship's documentation as they made their way to the video-phone and went through the process for re-entry into the United States. They understood the need for border security, but it always seemed odd to have so many different forms and identification to prove their U.S. citizenship. The process is complicated by the fact that the Departments of Immigration and Customs don't communicate, and each has separate entry requirements. The United States may have the Perry Victory Monument, but Canada has a better welcome.

The sound of steel drums drifted out of the Boathouse.

"How about we take a night off from boatgrub?" suggested Davis.

"You don't have to ask me twice," answered Beth.

The Boathouse has a number of food options. There's a sort of fast food court, an indoor dining room, and a party deck. After being in the sun all day, the McGowans took the higher-priced option and stayed indoors in the air conditioning. When the server came to the table, the menus were not really necessary. Jimmy Buffett's "Cheeseburger in Paradise" was echoing through the room and sounded like a perfect suggestion. Beth had bacon and American cheese on hers; Davis ordered his with mushrooms and Swiss. While they waited for their burgers, the waitress brought their drink order. It was Johnnie Walker Red on the rocks for Davis, and Beth had a glass of white Zinfandel.

By now Bob Marley was singing about peace in Africa, and Davis' eye caught the muted image on the flat screen TV in the corner. It was tuned to the news channel and subtitles rolled along the bottom of the screen. It was not the words that caught his eye; it was the onscreen image of a man in a business suit. It looked like Rad Finch, the president of Parker-Houston Investments. Just as he was about to say something to Beth, the white letters rolled across the screen: "Conrad Finch steps down from Parker-Houston. The Board of PHI did not confirm the value of his severance package, but estimates are that it is between eight-and-a half and nine-and-a half million dollars."

"Rad Finch is leaving PHI, and taking nine mil with him! Wow!"

Beth turned to see what Davis was talking about. She had only met Finch once. It was at a recognition dinner for one of the Boards that Davis served on when he was pastor at Covenant Church.

A new graphic replaced the image Finch on the monitor. It was a list of recent "Golden Parachutes." According to the chart, seven corporate firings in the last month totaled an estimated hundred-and-ten to a hundred twenty-three million dollars. Of course, these became losses to the corporations and to the stockholders.

"By that reckoning," said Davis, "PHI got off cheaply."

"You always thought he was a pretty good

leader, didn't you?" offered Beth.

"That was my impression, but how would I know? I just saw him in a volunteer capacity. We served on the same board, but obviously, we weren't in the same league. I've never been offered a thousand dollars as a severance, much less nine million. Then again, I've never been canned. Maybe I'm doing something wrong?"

"I don't think so," said Beth, and that ended all references to Conrad Finch and Dayton, Ohio.

** ** **

When the water taxi gently nudged against the hull of the boat, they felt like they had arrived home. Davis went below to boil some water for a cup of tea. Beth sat in the cockpit as the sinking sun surrendered the Bay to soft light and barn swallows swooping over the water to catch insects. That night they lay in their cabin listening to the sounds of reggae that, thankfully, ended around two in the morning when the party lights at the Boathouse dimmed.

The next morning came with mist over the water and a great blue heron wading along the sandbar at the far end of Gibraltar Island. The day's itinerary included six hours of sailing. They would follow the channel markers through the shallows between South Bass and Ballast Islands and then cut south around Kelley's Island and southeast across the shipping lanes into Sandusky Bay, pass Cedar Point and its roller coasters, and then hug the coast all the way to the Huron light and their home port.

After that there would be one more night on the boat, and three hours by car back to Fairborn and the house. Davis remarked that the six hours in the boat were always easier than three in the car. Beth agreed.

Chapter Four

At the Schuster

Since Jerry and Shelly lived in Beavercreek, the McGowans had agreed to meet them at the Fairfield Commons Mall so that they'd only have one car to park in downtown Dayton. First stop, however, was the Town and Country shops for an upscale pizza. The restaurant was famous for gourmet pizza, but in every other way it was a place for elegant dining. A hostess met them at the door and took their names for seating. Davis remarked that the line of people waiting to be seated seemed short, perhaps a sign of the local economic conditions. It was only five minutes when they heard the words, "McGowan, party of four, your table is ready."

They followed her lead into the dining area and to the left. They were seated in the greenhouse, an informal area with large hanging plants, rattan furniture, and a filtered view of the early evening sky. They settled in to look at the menus. Beth noticed that the pricing seemed far more reasonable than the Bendy Ditch Hotel.

"We took a little side trip to Elkhorn this summer," said Davis, after the server took their meal orders.

"The money capital of the world?" offered Jerry sarcastically.

Shelly gave him a sideways glance. "What did you think?"

"Well..." began Davis, "it sure didn't look like any other small town I've ever seen." Jerry smiled at the hesitation before Davis' carefully delivered words.

"That's because it isn't a normal place," Jerry added.

"No," said Beth, "it was a perfect little town, a picture book."

"Best little town that money can buy," was Ferguson's remark.

"Jerry and I have different reactions to Elkhorn," answered Shelly. "The place got under his skin very quickly. I had good years there. Now that we're away, I can see how really strange it was. It's so isolated that it's easy to lose perspective."

"When we drove in," said Beth, "I wondered why the place wasn't mobbed with tourists. It has all those quaint shops and ambiance. Then we went to the hotel for lunch."

Jerry laughed, "And you wondered how they could stay in business with prices like that!"

"Exactly," said Davis. "We thought we were back in Chicago at some swanky place on North Michigan Avenue!" The tension at the table fell to the floor and everyone laughed. "I have to admit, they didn't take to us very well. We were allowed to buy lunch and then they yanked away the welcome mat. I guess there was just no room in the inn, so to speak."

Beth explained about the desk clerk and how he seemed to remember Shelly fondly, but developed amnesia after lunch.

"Oh, that was Ronnie," said Shelly. "He's a good kid. His mother is one of the pillars of the church. He married his high school sweetheart and landed one of the best jobs in town."

"You mean the job of bouncer?" said McGowan. Jerry lost it again. This time Shelly smacked him on his knee.

"No, that's not fair," she said, mostly to Jerry. "When you live there and are on the inside, it makes sense. To an outsider, it's all different. Like I said, I was an insider and it was a gradual thing. Over time I understood the way things worked, and I just didn't question it. Ronnie is a townie. He lives in a nice house with a young, growing family. He makes a good living. If you drive anywhere within a fifty mile radius of Elkhorn, make that a hundred miles, and you won't find a cleaner, more prosperous town, and everyone there knows why. The Institute brings in clients, really important people. The town sees its job as taking care of the people from the Institute."

"And bouncing the riff-raff?"

"Well, mostly the prices do that!" she continued. "It does surprise me that Ronnie would say he didn't know me. Something else must have been going on there."

"Oh, he remembered you," said Davis. "He called you 'Reverend Shelly' before lunch and then changed your name and sex after. He thought I was talking about some guy named 'Sheldon Marvin' at the cable company."

"Well, that's completely bogus. The only ones working in the office at the cable company are Shad, Clark, and Vicky with a 'y'."

"It really is a small town if you can name them all off the top of your head," replied Beth.

"It's really two towns, the people of Bendy Ditch and the people of the Institute. They get along fine, but they really don't mix very much."

"The Institute people are in and out. They don't stay for more than a year or so, even the executives," offered Jerry. "All the pastoral care like funerals and hospital visits are for the townies."

"That's not entirely true," said Shelly. "Marlene Zeller came to me when her mother died, and I performed the wedding for Brandon."

"That was something else," interjected Jerry. "The groom's parents chartered a bus and took everyone to Chicago. Put everyone up in the Hilton for two nights, but that's what you get when you are the son of Rad Finch."

"Rad Finch? The same one that bailed from PHI?" asked Davis.

"Yep," said Jerry. "He's a proud alumnus of the great Elkhorn Institute."

"You do have friends in high places," chimed in Beth, "or, at least, some of them used to be in high places."

"Oh, a number of them are here in Dayton," spoke Shelly softly. "I had thought that, by now, at least one of them would have visited the church. Marlene Zeller is here. She's the CFO at Watermark Paper in Moraine. I had thought that we were particularly close."

"Well, ask them! They'll tell you that the guy you married led you astray," said Jerry. "They see your leaving as a betrayal, and that's my fault."

"No, I agreed with the move, and I have known for a long time that it was the right thing to do." The McGowans suddenly felt like they were eavesdropping on a private family matter.

"Maybe they don't know you're here in town. You've only been here a few months," suggested

Davis.

Shelly was silent for a moment before speaking. Her voice gave away the hurt that lingered beneath the surface. "I thought of that, but there was a big article in the Dayton Daily when we arrived. After all, a married couple coming as co-pastors of the flagship church is an unusual story."

"Especially when the guy is a real cowboy," chimed in Jerry.

Davis cleared his throat, "I was at Covenant Church for more than a decade, and they might want to dispute that flagship stuff!" The group laughed. "Ah, yes," added McGowan, "tall steeple politics! Makes me glad to be a lowly non-tenure track instructor! But you're right, you had good press coverage. No, St. Andrew's got great press!"

"And they are very busy people. So I called Marlene. Didn't get past her administrative assistant; however, I left a message. So far, nothing."

The food was served, and it was apparent that Martin and Ferguson were the more adventurous eaters. Beth had the closest thing to a plain pepperoni pizza as she could decipher from the descriptions on the menu, and Davis had a spinach quiche. Dinner seemed to pass quickly. The rest of the conversation steered clear of the Bendy Ditch, and was decidedly more lighthearted.

"We need to run," said Davis, taking out his

pocket watch to look at the time.

"And you tease me about my cowboy belt?" commented Jerry. "Nice watch, old man!" But Davis was right. They were still in Kettering and the Schuster was several miles away. Fortunately, the traffic was not heavy on Far Hills Avenue that time of the evening, and there were still available parking spaces in the lot just north of the Schuster Center on Main Street. They hurried down the sidewalk and entered from Main Street.

They were rushing as they walked through the lobby. Davis was sorry that they had not allowed more time. Dayton had done an excellent job in making a home for the arts. He had pointed out the Victoria Theater as they left the parking lot. That was the venue for performing arts; the Schuster was the home of the Philharmonic Orchestra.

They walked up the ramp to where a docent looked at their tickets and directed a waiting usher to show them to their seats. Shelly opened the program and was delighted to see that a chorus was joining the orchestra in Schubert's *Mass in A-Flat Major*. She spent even more time going over the list of patrons.

As the concert unfolded, Davis felt good about being able to introduce Shelly and Jerry to this bonus of life in Dayton. He squeezed Beth's hand. "Do you think they're enjoying this?"

"Oh, yes," replied Beth. He didn't really need her to tell him: he could see their reactions, still it was always good to be confirmed.

The evening slid by and soon the four were rising to leave. On the way back to the Main Street entrance, Shelly came to a sudden stop. She was looking toward a group of couples standing in the lobby. Davis recognized Rad Finch among them, and he looked none the worse for wear considering he had just been sacked. On the other hand, he had nine million reasons to be in a good mood.

In the same group was another person whom Davis recognized. William Slater and his wife, Elizabeth Carnaby, were chatting on the fringes of the huddle.

"There's the mayor," said McGowan to Ferguson as he gestured toward Slater. "Bill and I go way back. I'd introduce you, but I'm afraid he'd accuse you of keeping bad company."

Jerry laughed. "I wouldn't worry about it. The Elkhorn crowd would say the same of you if they saw us talking."

Suddenly Shelly left the three, walking purposely toward the tightly packed group. She touched one of the women on her right forearm to draw her attention. The woman turned; her face blushed instantly, and Davis could see that Shelly said something that drew the attention of the larger group. Rad Finch turned on her, and spoke through tightly drawn lips. Whatever he said spun Shelly around. By the time she reached Jerry and took his arm, tears were streaming down her face.

"Please, let's go home."

"I'll bet I could take him," said Jerry sounding more cowboy than parson.

"Let's just go home."

The car was silent for the most part as Davis took the ramp to the freeway out of town. Every few minutes, however, Shelly's breathing would quietly shudder. When they got back to the mall where Ferguson had parked his car, Shelly spoke.

"I have to apologize," she said. "This was a wonderful evening, and a delightful concert. I didn't expect to see that crowd of Institute people. I always thought of them as very good friends, and I... I just didn't see it coming. Thank you, both."

With that, Jerry and Shelly went to their own car and got in. The McGowans did not pull out immediately. Davis didn't want them to be stranded in the event that their car wouldn't start, but when it became clear that Jerry wasn't going to turn the key any time soon, he thought it best to leave.

"I guess they have some things to talk about," he said.

Chapter Five

Office Hours

"Dr. McGowan, can I come in?" A round-faced, bespectacled student poked his head through the open door of Davis' office. "I'm Ashton Zink. I'm in your nine-forty Religion 204 class."

"Yes," answered Davis, "you sit in the front row on the left hand side. How can I help you, Ashton?"

"I was wondering, Dr. McGowan, if you'd mind if I recorded your lectures. It will help me with my notes." He held up a small digital recorder.

"As long as it's only for your personal use, that's fine."

"Thanks, Dr. McGowan."

The head in the doorway disappeared and Davis turned his attention back to his desktop monitor. "That's impressive! The students want to record your every word, Professor!"

Davis looked up to see Shelly Martin standing in the doorway.

"Oh yes, one of my eager disciples," he answered mockingly. "But don't be too impressed," he said as he motioned her into the room to sit in the chair opposite him. "It isn't what you think, and keep your voice down with that 'professor' stuff. To the students all faculty look alike, but in academic corridors, that title 'professor' belongs to the higher-ups. I am just a lowly instructor who lives safely beneath the politics of academia."

"Still, you must be doing something right if students want to record you."

"No, it's really not that flattering. You see, it's still early in the quarter. I spoke with that young man on the first day of class. He told me then that he had a degree from a local Bible College. He was confident and assured. Once I began to speak, I could see his expression change. Evidently, I didn't say anything he expected. This happens every quarter. The ones who already know the Bible decide that I am the Devil Incarnate and they want to trap me speaking heresy. That goes on for about three weeks. Then I assign them a research project and send them to Dunbar Library. Once they read the reference books, they suddenly realize that I'm not making this stuff up. Hopefully, he'll be one of the students who come back to ask why he wasn't told any of this before."

"And what do you say?"

"I tell them that I don't know why churches stopped teaching the Bible and, instead, took up teaching a popularized, simple formula for salvation. This is a state school; I am not trying to win them over to a particular way of thinking, so I just tell them the truth. This is the history and the culture of the people who wrote the Bible. Whatever you choose to believe, you still have to deal with these realities."

"So, the recording may be used as evidence in your heresy trial?"

"The good news is that they no longer burn heretics! Speaking of burning, are you okay?"

"That's why I came today. I called and found out when you had office hours, and Jerry dropped me off. This is a big campus, and it took me awhile to find Millett Hall, especially in the rain."

"Is it raining? Ah, the advantage of having an office on this side of the hall. No windows! Every day is the same."

"I want to apologize, again. I was eleven years in Elkhorn, and to be rejected so absolutely, well, that was too much to handle."

Davis studied the woman who was sitting in front of him. Shelly looked to be about forty-five with short, dark hair. As always, she was neatly and professionally dressed. He could see in her manner that she probably didn't let people get too close to her until there was a foundation for trust. He knew that she had been through a lot, losing both parents at a young age, and a husband to Alzheimer's. Those people whom she allowed into her life were as precious to her as family. They were, in fact, her only family.

"I know the feeling," said Davis. "Ministers are professionals, but it's a profession that takes deep root in the self— at least it does with the good ones." During the ensuing silence Shelly looked around the room. Her eyes fell on a neatly lettered plaque:

> There are 10 kinds of people in the world,
> those who understand binary numbers,
> and those who don't.

"Okay," she said, "there's a story behind this."

"Not really. My father and one of my brothers are engineers and my sister is a mathematician. You can't be in my family without thinking in binaries. Sometimes in Philosophy class I write that on the board and see who gets it. The people who get it aren't any smarter; they just bring a different experience to seeing it. On a good day, it becomes a discussion; on a bad day, I have to sing and dance."

"The Elkhorn Institute people had a different saying. They'd say, 'There are two kinds of people in the world, those who can afford to retire and those who only think they can.'"

"What was that about?"

"Money. It's like Jerry says, all value is measurable in dollars. That's why he was so pissed at them when they tried to 'buy him out,' as he calls it. He had been in Miller as long as I had been in Elkhorn and was really troubled by the fact that they seemed to think that loyalty is a market-driven commodity."

"What's your schedule like today?" asked Davis, looking at his watch.

"I am taking a personal sanity day. Jerry suggested it. In fact, he dropped me off at the student center. If we had known that Millett was clear across campus, we would have driven around more or, at least, brought better rain gear."

"No," said Davis, "what you really needed to know is that all the buildings at Wright State are connected by a system of tunnels."

"Oh," said Shelly. "You mean that I could have avoided the wet feet and soggy umbrella?"

"Completely! I have a class in a few minutes. If you could stick around for an hour or so, we can grab some lunch and talk. If Jerry's available, there's a nice sandwich shop in the student center where he dropped you off. There's visitor parking there as well."

"Can I sit in on your class?"

"Officially, no! Only registered students and auditors are permitted. But unofficially, sure! The department is always looking for qualified people who might be able to teach in the future. Maybe you'd like to try your hand at teaching some day. Who knows, maybe you'll end up teaching here as an adjunct. That's how I got started. How much do you know about Hinduism?"

"Just a little bit less than nothing."

"Then I see no reason that you can't attend. Today, I am going to use an example from Hindu art, and I'm sure it will amount to baby-talk compared to what my colleagues teach. I'm counting on the fact that you won't unmask my fraud to them by blabbing about my ignorance."

"So, you do worry about being caught in heresy; it's just Hindu, rather than Presbyterian, authority that you fear. Dr. McGowan, may I record your presentation?"

"Now I am afraid!"

"Davis, cowboy-up!"

"Well, at least you didn't tell me to 'put on your big girl panties and deal with it'."

Chapter Six

Ganesha

While McGowan's classes had no assigned seating, students generally sat in the same place week after week. Davis told Shelly to take any seat she wanted. There were a few vacant spots and the class would adjust.

This particular class was not one of McGowan's favorites to teach. In the catalogue, the course was entitled "What is Religion?" It was not that he thought the topic inappropriate, but he had personal misgivings. After so many years in the parish, returning to the world of academics was both challenging and refreshing. This class was one that forced him to stretch his thinking. It was an area where he felt less qualified to teach than in other departmental offerings. His presentations were meant to highlight certain universal elements of some of the major world religions, and Davis felt that there were too many gaps in his knowledge. As a result, he structured his presentations on the sociology of religion and used stories from many religions to illustrate the point. Today, he would talk about his favorite Hindu deity, Ganesha.

The context was a lecture illustrating some of the difficulties in understanding other cultures. Most of his students had never traveled too far from Ohio and the adjacent states, and he was teaching literature that came from cultures halfway around the world. On the other hand, Wright State had a lot of foreign students. More than once he told his class about a student who came forward after class with a confused look on his face.

"The way you describe the Bible sounds more like the way it is in Africa," he said. "I am from Togo, and Abraham's family seems more like my tribe than an American family."

Davis could only smile. "Yes," he said, "you are right. It's the American students who don't understand."

"In my country," he continued, "if I want a passport, I go to the government. For something important, like I want to get married, I go to my Chief." Here was a student who understood that not all ideas about government and authority crossed between cultures. Americans are brought up to believe that governments rule and hold power. Not all peoples have that same prejudice. Davis would confuse most of the class when he'd point out that in some countries various ethnic groups would claim different nationalities.

"He who doesn't visit thinks mother the only cook," began Davis. "It's an African proverb. We all grow up thinking that the way we think and do things is just like everyone else. It is not.

"Today, I am going to tell you about Ganesha, a favorite elephant-headed Hindu deity. I have a picture of him." With this, Davis projected a slide on the screen at the front of the class. "He's quite handsome, don't you agree?" The image showed what looked like the body of a six-armed human with an elephant head. Around Ganesha's waist was a serpent, and he was seated in the lotus position on the back of a rat.

Some sniggers ran through the room.

"Don't laugh," said McGowan, "this guy is great! His story began when Shiva's wife, Parvati, wanted to have a child, but Shiva had been distracted. Parvati, being clever, created a boy from the dirt that she scraped off her own body. Of course, when Shiva came home he did what a lot of us do, he reacted first, before asking any questions. Why shouldn't he? After all, he knew that he wasn't the father, so he cut off the young man's head. When Parvati explained that this was her child, and hers alone, not the product of some illicit affair, something had to be done. The gods told Ganesha to go into the jungle and take the head of the first animal that he sees lying on the ground with his head facing north. Well, there you go! The first animal he sees is an elephant and that's why Ganesha is a boy with an elephant head.

"But there's more with Ganesha. He has quite a sweet tooth and likes cakes. One night he was stuffing himself with sugary rice-balls. After eating his fill, he went riding off on his trusty rat which ended up tripping on a snake. Ganesha was thrown off, and– this is the graphic part– his belly split open and the rice-balls popped out. Undeterred, Ganesha stuffed the sweets back into his belly and used the snake as a belt to hold himself together. Of course, the moon saw all of this and laughed at Ganesha, so he ripped off one of his tusks and heaved it at the moon. Ever since, the moon has not been able to remain full for more than a day or two. That's a true story."

McGowan paused.

"I want to show you another picture." He opened a different file on the podium PC, and the image of Ganesha was replaced with a more realistic painting from the fifteenth century.

"This is entitled, 'The Annunciation with John the Baptist and Saint Andrew'. It's an example of western art. Let me introduce the characters. This is Mary, the mother of Jesus," he said pointing to one of the figures. On one knee before her was a long-haired young man offering a lily to the seated woman. "The fellow kneeling is the angel Gabriel and, here on the left is John the Baptist, and on the right is Andrew, the disciple.

"The picture has a lot of symbolism built in, but I just want you to look at the figures. They look human, don't they? Now look at Ganesha." Davis clicked back to the previous slide. "Does he look human?" Everyone was shaking their heads.

"Which seems more believable, and why?"

A brave soul spoke quietly from the front row, "The picture of Mary."

"Did everyone hear that? The Italian painting seems more believable than the Hindu art." Heads bobbed in agreement.

"Why?"

"They look like people."

"They do, don't they?" said Davis. "Even the angel looks human. He has wings, but otherwise isn't very startling. The painting doesn't seem alien." He switched back to the drawing of Ganesha. "And this one doesn't seem real?

"Actually, what you are noticing is one of the differences between eastern and western art. What if I told you that the person who drew Ganesha intentionally made him as unrealistic as possible? It's like the artist is saying here's my picture of Ganesha, he's real but don't believe the picture! He's not real in the way the picture shows him."

Confused faces looked back at Davis.

"The artist is saying this fellow is one of our divinities; his story is true, but I don't want you to think that it is literally true. What we have here is art that is intentionally alien. It is meant to push the imagination beyond the normal. It is an abstract idea in picture form.

"Ganesha is the consummate survivor. He is innovative and positive in the face of unintended and unforeseen events. The Ganesha story is a reminder that you are not in control, and events will not play out the way you imagine. Everything has unintended consequences, and the test is whether or not those bitten by them can take them in stride. We should have paid attention to Ganesha when we invaded Iraq. The assumption was that our troops would be hailed as liberators, but we were thrown off our mounts. If that happened to Ganesha, he would adjust and survive. Took us a lot longer to figure that what we intended and what happened were two different things. That's Ganesha, and the artist won't let you confuse the crazy image with the real experience of life. The experience of the unexpected, now that's what's real!"

** ** **

"I've seen the pictures of the elephant boy," said Shelly, "but I never knew the story. He's the master of the unintended consequence."

"That's the way I understand it," answered Davis, "but I don't claim to know much about eastern religion, and I'm sure that there are people in my department who might take exception to my Ganesha lounge act!"

The two were going down the central stairwell in Millett Hall. When they reached the lowest level, light streamed in from the right hand corridor. "That's the way to the outside parking lot exit," said Davis, "but we want to go this way." He indicated left, and they made a U-turn. In the space of ten feet the vinyl floor tile ended and they were walking on what looked like a polished roadway of battleship gray.

"Welcome to the underworld!" said Davis. "Wright State was specifically designed to allow accessibility for students and faculty with disabilities. The result is that we have our own underground highway system." It was true. The passages were wide enough to allow electric vehicles to pass carrying supplies from building to building.

When she'd walked across campus in the rain, Shelly had seen only a few people with umbrellas and most were walking from the parking area. Now she understood why. The underground corridors were teeming with students. Along one passage there was a large cart with a coffee vendor. Near a set of elevator doors were study desks and the signs indicated an active wireless network for computer access.

Suddenly, they crossed over a wide threshold, and they were in a building with classrooms and offices on either side of the hallway.

"It would be easy to get lost down here," noted Shelly.

"After a while it's easy," answered Davis. "It's the same as the quad areas above. We're in the basement of University Hall right now. If you think it's nice on rainy days, it's even better in winter." Just then a whirring sound behind them grew louder. Davis took Shelly's arm and stepped aside to allow a motorized wheelchair to pass.

"That's pretty neat," said Shelly.

"It gives some students a lot of freedom," agreed Davis. "When the tunnels are nearly empty, you really have to watch. I think some of those wheelchairs are souped-up for speed."

After a few more twists and turns, Davis directed Shelly to a flight of stairs. "I usually take the stairs, but there's an elevator around the corner if you'd rather not walk."

"Stairs are fine."

At the top of the stairs was the first floor hallway

of the Student Center. Shelly looked out the glass doors and saw Millett Hall on the far side of the campus. "We go this way," said Davis, directing her to the interior of the building.

"It's too bad that Jerry can't join us," said Davis.

"He'll be here in a bit," answered Martin. "He's meeting someone from the Presbytery for lunch, but he should be here around one-thirty."

Davis went through the sandwich line, and Shelly bought a salad. After they were both served, he led the way back into a quiet area that was isolated from where the majority of the students were eating.

"We'll be able to talk here," said Davis, indicating a table in one corner.

"I think that you were telling that Ganesha story for me today."

Davis laughed. "Honestly, it's in the syllabus and I didn't know that you were going to be here!"

"Well, it doesn't matter. It fits what I've been going through. When I left Elkhorn, I obviously set off some sort of chain reaction. I mean, the way I am being treated isn't normal and it isn't random. Last night– that group of people at the Schuster, I knew them all."

"I recognized Rad Finch, but not the others," said Davis.

"I knew them all. I know them all. I can tell you

their kids' names; I can tell you their pets' names! I went over to Marlene Zeller and said, 'Is this a meeting of the EBC?' and Finch blasts me: 'What did you say, and who the hell are you?'"

"I don't understand, what is 'EBC'?" asked Davis.

"It's one of the Institute's pet acronyms. It stands for the 'Empty Box Club.' They are a secretive group, but every once in a while a door would open a crack. Marlene explained it to me once when we were friends, but that was before Ganesha rode in on his rat!"

Davis laughed. It was meant to ward off Shelly's sense of hurt over the events of the previous night.

"Anyway," she continued, "and, apparently this is really a hot item in the Institute's jargon. An empty box is something that you can sell for a lot of money. You can even sell it more than once. You can sell empty boxes at higher and higher prices, and no one knows that they are holding something worthless until they open the box. The one who opens the box is the loser because he or she has nothing to sell or pass on."

"Okay," said Davis, "I suppose that means something."

"It must! Otherwise, why would Finch be so upset last night? I only knew it by accident. The reason Marlene told me in the first place was because of a silly thing that was said at a small group Christmas party, at the Finch's house, no less. It was one of those fun things where everyone is supposed to wrap some inexpensive gift and bring it to exchange. Everyone draws a number from a hat and then that determines the order that you get to choose a gift from the pile. You can either choose a gift from under the tree or take one away from someone else. Basically, the last person to choose gets first choice."

"Every church I've been in has someone that suggests that game," said Davis. "I hated it. It's just mean."

"I'm not a fan either, but somewhere during the scrabble over boxes, Ken Cousins said, 'I'll bet Rad has already emptied all the boxes anyway.' Everybody really laughed. I thought it was funny, but not that funny. The next day Marlene told me the inside joke. Evidently, some part of the strategy at the Institute has to do with selling empty boxes."

"I must be missing something here. Does that make any sense? What does the Elkhorn Institute do besides bankroll an over-priced small town?"

"That's the big question. I was there for eleven years and I have to admit that I really don't know."

"Pardon my denominational prejudice, but what Methodist minister stays anywhere for eleven years?"

"It does sound suspicious, doesn't it? At times I thought it was because my husband was so ill that the District Superintendent felt sorry for me and didn't want to make me move. That might have been it, but only in part. These people have ways of getting what they want. That's why they really were angry when Jerry and I found a position here in Dayton where we could be co-pastors."

"You'd think that they'd be happy for you both. You had a long tenure there, and, after all, they're professionals; they know about career advancement."

"I think it was even more basic than that. They wanted me to stay in Elkhorn, and they would have been happy if Jerry wanted to stay in Elkhorn. They didn't want us living in Pierre and commuting. They wanted us living and working in town, period. It was that simple. It was about geography."

"But what difference would that make?"

"I don't know," she said softly, "but you asked me what the Institute did." Her voice became animated, "I can tell you what it didn't! I never saw any advertised seminars or continuing education opportunities. I never saw any course descriptions. Over eleven years, I have met most of the CEO's of the major corporations and investment houses. They all passed through little Elkhorn, South Dakota, and, as far as I know, not one of them remembers my name.

Sorry, but I don't think I am that forgettable."

"Trust me, you're not," said Davis. "But you think that you and Jerry were supposed to stay in Elkhorn so that you wouldn't see six of them together at the Schuster Center in Dayton, Ohio."

"Right now," she added, "that makes as much sense as anything. If we had moved to DC, it would have been to 'not see' a group of them huddled together at the Kennedy Center. I can link them all to Elkhorn, and for some reason that's not supposed to happen. The point is that this isn't about Dayton. I'd bet I'd find a group from Elkhorn in any population center where I would go. When I left, I screwed something up! When Jerry and I left Elkhorn, we caused some kind of unintended consequence."

"Enter, Ganesha," said Davis.

"Enter, Ganesha," agreed Shelly.

They looked up to see Jerry approaching. "You two seem lost in conversation," he said.

"Speaking of unintended consequences," said Davis.

"What?" asked Ferguson.

"I'll tell you later, Dear," said Shelly with a smile.

Chapter Seven

Web Search

The rain had stopped, and Davis took the fresh air route back to Millett Hall and his third floor office. It was not his practice to do any personal web surfing from his University computer, but today he would make an exception. He entered the words "Elkhorn Institute" in the search engine window on his University homepage. Immediately, several thousand hits including the words "Elkhorn" and "institute" came up on the screen. He narrowed the search by putting quotation marks around the title. He had only one hit, and it was the corporate site.

"That's very odd," he said to no one but himself. "If all those bigwigs have been to this place, you'd think the name would appear on a lot of résumés." He clicked on the link.

He was puzzled by what came up on the screen. It was a very vanilla, static site. There wasn't any logo or photo of the grand exterior of the building he had seen on the banks of the Bendy Ditch. In fact, there was no mention of the town of Elkhorn other than in the name of the institute. The sum of the writing on the web page matched the sign on the exterior of the building: "Elkhorn Management Institute, Architects of Free Enterprise." In the lower right hand corner was a small link that said: "contact us." Davis clicked the link and went to an equally plain page that gave only a post office box in Sioux Falls and an email link. He clicked the mailto link and his browser opened to create a message using his faculty address.

Davis hesitated, and then he began to type:

Greetings: I am Dr. Davis McGowan, a member of the Department of Philosophy at Wright State University in Dayton, Ohio. I am currently writing selected management schools to see what seminars are available in the area of business management ethics. To this point, my studies have been in philosophical ethics and I wish to experience the teaching of ethics from a business/professional point of view. If the Elkhorn Management Institute has such a program, I would appreciate your direction in submitting an application. Thank you.

He thought for a moment before sending the message. Then with a click, it was gone. He contin-

ued his investigation by searching the Internet for all
references to Conrad Finch, Marlene Zeller, and
Kenneth Cousins. Shelly probably had many more
names, but these three would suit his purposes.
Each search produced a lot of hits. Unlike the Institute, these people were well-documented on the
web. Naturally, they were listed as officers in their
corporate roles, but they also had a miscellany of
honorary degrees, memberships on boards of trus-
tees, and keynote speeches before professional or-
ganizations. For all their status, none had ever listed
"Elkhorn Institute" on anything.

According to the Parker-Houston Investments'
site, Rad Finch had come directly from the leadership of a Chicago-based securities house. If Shelly
was telling the truth, there must have been a two or
three year gap during the time in South Dakota, but
that was buried somewhere in the time line. The
same was true for Zeller and Cousins. There were no
gaps in their official résumés, but no mention of
years spent in Elkhorn, either.

Davis began to write another message, this time
to Shelly Martin:

> Shelly, I've been searching the web for
> news about the Institute and about Cous-
> ins, Zeller, and Finch. Nothing adds up.
> It's like the place doesn't exist, except we

both know that it does! Something about you has them scared. We could leave it at that, or try to unravel the fact that they think you know more than you know! (Is that double-talk?) Obviously, they didn't like your reference to empty boxes. They must suddenly be aware that you heard things in social settings that describe whatever they are up to. If you need someone to bounce ideas around with… well, I'm your mentor! Davis

McGowan turned his attention to the work at hand; he had the first drafts of student papers to grade. He opened the first and read the opening sentence, "According to Webster…" He always warned students about the idea of leading with Webster.

"When you are writing a research paper at this level," he would tell them, "your reader already knows how the word is used in modern English. You are trying to explain how these concepts were understood in an ancient culture. A modern English dictionary won't help you there!"

He could already feel the pain of a bad paper, "I don't care what Webster says," he said aloud, "you are in college, not high school!"

He was delivered from his agony by a message from Shelly Martin. It came so quickly, that he knew she had to be sitting at her computer:

The more I think about all their inside jokes and innuendos, I am as puzzled and curious as you are! After our conversation at lunch, I remembered a bunch of other one-liners from that Christmas party. Here are a few:

"I'm sure one of these boxes has a parachute... "

"Face it, the last thing anyone takes from a box is a parachute..."

"Knowing Rad, he doesn't keep his in the box, he wears it under his jacket!" (They really laughed at that!)

Then there was this one: "Empty boxes don't stink!"

Your guess is as good as mine! Maybe you can figure it out! I never thought of this stuff as having any other purpose than the banter between friends. No wonder that I can't understand it. With

the way they treat me now, maybe we
never were friends.
- Shel

Davis wrote a one sentence reply: "What do
you know about their politics?"

Chapter Eight

Politics of War

While Davis was intrigued by Shelly's predicament, he had troubles of his own. In his teaching of the Bible, he was always looking for contemporary illustrations to help students distinguish between cultural patterns of east and west. While his years as a pastor made him leery of talking about politics, his descriptions of ancient Middle Eastern tribalism sounded like commentary on current events. He realized this in 2001 as tensions mounted just prior to the war in Afghanistan. One morning on the way to the University, he had heard on a news report that the Taliban would not surrender Osama bin Laden who had been implicated in the 9-11 collapse of the Twin Towers. Specifically, the commentator quoted the Taliban leaders who stated that bin Laden was a "guest" in their country. That day, as an aside, McGowan spoke about the Middle Eastern virtue of hospitality and the obligation of a host to protect his guests even if the guest were a total stranger seeking shelter.

The story had biblical parallels in Genesis. At the end of the lecture he added, "I don't think the Afghans can surrender bin Laden. To their way of thinking, our government is asking them to do something obscene."

A week later, the bombing of Afghanistan began. A student, who had seemed disinterested a week earlier, came to Davis after class and asked, "How come you're the only one who knew that?"

"A lot of people know this stuff," he protested, "but I can't say why it hasn't been taken into account."

From that time forward, it was easy to delineate cultural parallels between events in biblical times and news reports. Blood revenge was a case in point. For western officials, the unfortunate killing of innocent civilians was "collateral damage." To the families of the deceased, the injustice obligated the living to seek "blood revenge." So Coalition Forces were forced to try and distinguish between enemy forces and grieving family members under an obligation of honor.

At some point, an anonymous student wrote to the chair of the Religion Department requesting that Dr. McGowan give a faculty lecture on how the study of biblical culture sheds light on the wars in Iraq and Afghanistan.

"Of course, you are part of the non-tenured faculty and not required to give these community lectures," said Denton Barstow, the chair of the department, "but, if you are willing, it would be welcomed."

"I really don't think that I'm as much of a scholar as the regular faculty," Davis answered, "but I think I'm good at putting things in plain terms. Maybe it's from all those years of sermon illustrations."

"Whatever the reason, students respect your views and you do communicate well. May I put you on the schedule?"

During a weak moment, Davis had said, "Yes," knowing that he had months to prepare. But now the months were whittled down to two hours.

At four-thirty, Davis took the elevator to the first floor lounge where rows of chairs had been arranged facing a makeshift podium. The Dean and Dr. Barstow were already there along with a handful of students, mostly from his current classes.

"I guess this is really going to happen," he said approaching his two colleagues. He had only met the Dean on a few occasions, but she had always addressed Davis by name and supported the faculty lecture series.

"This is beyond the call of duty," said Dr. Ellen Harston. "I was just saying to Denton that these presentations really give our students insight as to how faculty members process information to inform opinion. I am looking forward to hearing what you have to say."

Davis was also wondering what he was going to say when he heard his name being spoken. Dr. Barstow had finished his introduction, and McGowan found himself walking toward the lectern.

His opening comments were rehearsed and drew a laugh which relaxed the room and calmed Davis' nerves. He spoke about many of the common biblical themes like hospitality and family/tribal identities before getting to the central point.

"Wars, when you think about them," he said, "follow a prescribed set of assumptions. I'm not just talking about the rules of engagement or the Geneva Convention. But even those tell you right away that there are prescribed rules within a given family of nations that share the same cultural beliefs. Where do these assumptions come from? The simple answer is from treaties or laws or common experiences."

Davis was losing the group, so he switched gears.

"Suppose someone you don't know very well invited you for dinner. What would you do? Maybe take a bottle of wine, not you students, you'd have to take vitamin water or something." Chuckles broke out.

"Walking into the house, what would you expect? Tables and chairs? Plates and utensils? The smell of food cooking? What if there was none of that? What if, when you got there, your host asked, 'Did you bring the food?'

"Now this is a foolish example, but it illustrates the point that the most basic elements in our lives could be very different if we were raised in a place with a different set of customs.

"I used to live in Western Pennsylvania. An Iranian family with small children and a new baby moved in across the street. We were having a really cold winter. One night I woke up because I thought I had heard a loud noise. You know how that goes, something wakes you up suddenly and you don't really know if something happened or if it was something you were dreaming? I looked at the clock and the clock face was dark. The power had gone out. What I had heard was a transformer blowing out from the cold.

"Good citizen that I am, I called the power company, and then I went and lit a fire in the fireplace to keep the house warm until the power came back on. I could look down the street and see all the lights out. I wasn't too worried about my neighbors; most everyone had a fireplace, but not Amir and his family. By seven-thirty it was getting colder, so I phoned over to the new neighbors saying, 'We have a fireplace. If you want to bring the baby and stay here until the power is restored you are more than welcome.'

"He said, 'No, thank you! That is generous, but we have a portable kerosene heater.' That was that, until the next spring. The neighbors got together for a picnic and everyone was there. When I went out on the patio, Amir's wife came and knelt down in front of me and started to talk about my great kindness to open my house to strangers. She told me that they had telephoned family in Iran the next day to tell them about their wonderful, virtuous neighbors! I had crossed a boundary that I had not seen. To me, it was no big deal. To them, it was a very big deal.

"The reason that boundaries cannot be seen is that we are preconditioned by our culture to see things in a very narrow way. 'War' is one of those things.

"Bin Laden said he was taking on the economic superpower. He was going to wage war. We know what war is, right? You attack and counterattack. The decisive wars end in victory; the indecisive ones end in stalemate.

"Isn't that correct? What if one side does not want to win? If that seems insane, it's because a cultural line has been crossed and we are in a new world where things are perceived differently. If bin Laden doesn't want anything from us except non-interference, if the cultural victory that he wants is that Islamic states will no longer be westernized, then the outcome of the war that he wants is not a military victory. All he needs is for us to give up! But why would we do that? Now this is the political divide that splits our nation and it's characterized negatively both ways. Neither the hawks nor the doves, however, seem to get it. All the talk is about the fighting. From the other side of the culture gap, the war is not about the fighting; it is economic. You don't defeat the U.S. by force; you defeat us by getting us to wage our war in our traditional, culturally defined way. Here's how it works. I send in a believer with twenty-five dollars of improvised explosive, and you send in a two million dollar Predator missile. Boom! You win! Right?

"Only on the battlefield! In the economic war, I am ahead by \$1,999,975. I can win a lot more; I just have to keep you shooting. Eventually, your free market economy will fall, and you will leave me alone. That's an image of war based on cultural differences.

"I really feel uncomfortable talking politics, so let me make it simple and unemotional, but cleverly devious. I'm sure you've all played the Hasbro board game, Monopoly. (Before it was a computer game, it was a board game; everybody sat on the floor... okay, I'm talking like an old person!) There is a cultural setting for that game and it's written on the inside of the box lid. It's called 'the rules,' and the winner is the one who has the most money when the other players declare bankruptcy. Suppose, however, that I introduce a cultural shift. You and I are playing against each other. But there's also a third player in our game. It's an invisible economic player who isn't actually there. We call her 'the banker.' In the real game, the banker is fairly benign. She holds title to properties until purchased; she collects fines, makes change, and gives you money for successfully going around in a circle. In my cultural shift I am going to add one more function to Ms. Banker. From now on, she has a special service. Whenever there is any property damage from a bad tenant, she arranges for repair to the property so that you can charge full rent for the next renter who lands on your square. (Since there are only two of us, that would be me!)

"Let me warn you, in this game, I am going to be a terrorist tenant. You charge me twelve dollars for rent, but I am going to leave garbage in the back hall and you'll have to pay fourteen dollars to have the mess cleaned up. I am terrible. Once I took all the copper tubing out of the basement and sold it as scrap metal. I tell you, you'd be better off not charging me rent! I get mad playing by your stinking rules. I decide that I don't even want to own any property in your materialistic world. Pretty soon, you own everything, and you gloat when you take my rent money. It seems like the shortest game in history. I purchase no property and always pay you the rent until I have nothing. Who won?

"I have zero, and the banker informs you that the repair bills were 125% greater than all the money you collected as rent. It turns out that my having zero dollars is a much better economic position than the total of your debt to the banker. In other words, I win! I have more than you. You thought you had value in those little boxes you called houses, but I had silently emptied the box!"

Davis' words echoed through his mind at the

very moment they came out of his mouth. "You win the game if the other guy is only holding an empty box."

The response to the lecture was heartening. Though his presentations were not academically sweet, it was his lounge act that made him a success in the classroom. In another way, however, this presentation made him think very differently about Shelly's problem. He had not crossed over the Rubicon, but he felt that he had forded the Bendy Ditch.

Chapter Nine

Fall Frenzy

The next two weeks were filled with term papers and student conferences. Jerry and Shelly were even busier trying to satisfy all the social obligations that followed their arrival in a new congregation. As an outsider, Davis had been impressed by their priorities from the very beginning. Within two weeks of their arrival, the pair had visited all the homebound and terminally ill members. From a physical standpoint, these were the most vulnerable people in the parish, and a visit from the new pastors confirmed the message of compassion that came from the pulpit. Some pastors were more like politicians who succeeded by playing to the powerbrokers. The shut-ins did not fit that category. They were not particularly wealthy or influential contributors, nor did they speak out or complain at congregational meetings. They were invisible to the average church member. Jerry and Shelly's first act, however, was to affirm their humanity.

In terms of the continuing rifts between Shelly and her former parishioners, things seemed to be settling down. After the initial shock at the Schuster, the daily requirements of career pushed further inquiry to a lower priority. Davis did receive two emails which continued to haunt the private moments of his thoughts just before falling asleep. One email was Shelly's quick response to his inquiry about the personal politics of the Elkhorn set.

"They never seemed to be oriented to one party or the other," she wrote. "I say that, but it was always clear that they preferred a small government with no regulatory interests. You'd think that they'd have been gung-ho Republican, but I think it was more like they would have a strategy for whoever was in power, and they kept options open. They were very cynical about Washington. When they'd get on a roll they'd banter things like: 'Congress can't actually do anything, but it can stop things from getting done!' They would also say that to an elected representative 'long range planning' meant 'until the next election' and 'It's cheaper to buy a politician than to run a thirty second Super Bowl ad.' Finch once said that 'Contributions are always welcome, but bribes get smelly after a time.' If I think of more, I'll let you know. BTW, did you catch the news about the CEO of Borkman-Reeves announcing that they were going to honor executive bonuses even though the company was going belly-up? That guy always sat in the second row on Christmas and Easter. (But I bet he doesn't remember me!)"

The second email was actually a notification of a failed email delivery. After two days, Davis received a message indicating that his server was unable to transmit his message to the Elkhorn Institute. "Those usually come back in seconds or minutes," he said under his breath.

Acting on intuition, he returned to the site where he had found the email link. He found himself looking at an error message: "NOT FOUND. The requested URL http:// was not found on this server."

** ** **

The change from summer to fall is colorfully heralded across the northeastern states. Ohio's foliage change varies somewhat based on the rainfall so that the timing of the seasonal change is not nearly as constant as the reappearance of King Kong on the roof of the costume shop in Fairborn, Ohio. It was an annual ritual in a town that loves to celebrate Halloween.

The McGowans now called the city of Fairborn their home even though they were relative newcomers to that Dayton area suburb. As Davis saw it, the town had grown up around the chain link fence that marked the perimeter of Wright Patterson Air Force Base. Actually, it had begun as two distinct towns, Fairfield and Osborn. While the name "Fairfield" survived on road signs and in a shopping mall, the town itself disappeared when Osborn marched across a field to join it. Technically, the town didn't march *per se*; it was dragged on flatbeds when the engineers created flood plains to avert disasters like the one that had decimated Dayton in 1913. In response to the Great Flood, as it was called, city leaders proposed a passive system of dams that would slow the flow of water on its rush downstream toward Dayton. Osborn, sitting low on the land, was one of the casualties of that plan. With the construction of the Huffman Dam on the Mad River, the small cluster of buildings was in potential flood danger. The solution was to move them closer to Fairfield. In the early fifties, the two contiguous towns became one. The villages had already been joined-at-the-hip, so to speak, so the name of the new city became a merger of the older monikers.

In some ways, this "new" town became frozen in time. Many homes became rental properties for airmen stationed at the base. In the more recent past, students would flock into apartments and townhouses as an alternative to dormitory living at Wright State. The hospital at Wright-Patt made the area attractive to retiring military personnel who received medical services as a part of their pension.

Keeping businesses in business is difficult for older communities whose traffic flow has been hijacked by interstates and regional malls. Fairborn's first line of defense is Halloween. Buildings and shops that have not been remodeled since the nineteen fifties remain reminders of a simpler time and provide an evening of free entertainment for families preparing for the haunting eve before All Saints Day.

Beth and Davis walked three blocks from their home to take in the festival atmosphere. Speakers hanging from the lamp posts blared out monster-mashing music served up from the past. People were shopping at the old Five and Dime, one of three costume shops, or the comic book store. The McGowans were mostly looking at the costumes and displays of ghosts, gravestones, and oversized inflatable characters that looked down from the rooftops.

"Can you imagine this going on in Hatteras?"

asked Beth.

Davis thought for a moment about the small town on the Ohio River where the local Church of God lambasted all the satanic shortcomings of the secular world. "No, I can't," he answered. "Here, it's what keeps these businesses alive."

As he was speaking, voices called from behind, "Beth, Davis!" It was Jerry Ferguson. He and Shelly quickened their pace to join the McGowans.

"Welcome to haunted Fairborn," said Davis. "A minister with a good 'fire and brimstone' sermon could do a real killing here!"

"I think someone already has," answered Jerry, "one of the store windows back there is full of body parts. I have to say, however, that the hand does resemble a latex glove and the 'guts' look like vermicelli."

"Add a few apples for bobbing, and you've got a church youth group Halloween party," said Beth.

"Now, that is scary," added Shelly.

"How have you two been?" asked Davis.

"No problems, or maybe no new problems," said Shelly. "The congregation keeps us both busy, but, so far, it's been very good. Have you ever noticed how some of the really sick people seem to hold on until the new pastor gets on the scene?"

Davis thought back to his first year as a young pastor in Hatteras. That first year, he conducted twenty-four funerals in a congregation of fewer than five hundred. "Yes, I remember that well. I think, particularly with the older folk, that the church has been such a part of their lives that they don't want to be buried by some guest minister. They do seem to wait."

"Happened to me when I first went to Miller, too," said Jerry. "Of course, some of it has to do with the fact that the funeral directors see the new guy in town as the one to ask for the funerals of the non-churchgoers."

"Have you had a chance to look around?" asked Beth.

"We've pretty much seen it all," said Shelly. "In fact, Jerry decided to go for a whole new look and bought some things at the variety store."

"Let me guess, a mask? Probably Cheney, Bush, or Obama," Davis replied.

"I'm shocked," said Jerry mockingly, "shocked that you think I would stoop to the level of politics. I did buy a mask, but one that has a long literary heritage."

Beth laughed out, "Frankenstein's Monster!"

"Oh, she's good," said Jerry, "and, I bought this great ball cap that has a ponytail attached. I can wear it to road rallies when I get my Harley."

"Like that's going to happen!" announced Shelly.

"Anyway," said Beth in an attempt to retrieve the conversation from the banter, "if you aren't in a hurry, why don't we go back to our house for a cup of coffee or something?"

"I'd prefer tea," said Shelly.

"And, I'd rather have a beer," said Jerry. Shelly gave him a sideways glance. "What?" he said. "I'm not a Methodist; I never took the pledge."

Davis laughed. "We can handle both! After all, I'm a Presbyterian, too."

The walk to the house was a pleasant interlude. Davis had time to speak with Shelly while Jerry and Beth walked a little ahead.

"I haven't been saying much to Jerry," she confided. "He gets protective of the whole situation. But, a few days ago I received a call at the church. The caller wouldn't give her name when the secretary asked, but asked for me specifically and called me Shelly. When I picked up the phone, there was a pause and then whoever it was said 'I am so sorry,' and hung up. I think it was Marlene Zeller."

"Whew," said Davis, "what does that mean? Is she sorry for what happened at the Schuster? If that's the case, why didn't she identify herself?"

"I don't know. Anyway, I want you to know that I'm trying to pull together some notes. Lists and photos mostly. Every time I hear a business report on TV these days, I hear the name of someone I know."

"But they don't know you, and they never went to the Elkhorn Institute, and that place doesn't actually exist," added Davis.

"Bizarre, isn't it? That place was real to me for eleven years. It would still be real if I were there now, but I'm here, now. Well, I don't want to upset Jerry, but I am just making a list of names of people who passed through the non-existent town."

"Fair enough."

"What are you two talking about back there?" asked Jerry.

"Mostly boring minister stuff that cowboys wouldn't understand," Davis bandied back. "Hey, are you two going up to Kirkmont for Presbytery?" Every October the regional meeting of the Presbyterian Church was held at the denomination's summer camp in Zanesfield.

"I am," answered Jerry, "but Shelly is too busy. She's leading a discussion at a women's study circle. I think I lucked-out on that one, but I'm not sure that I can even find the place."

"I'll tell you what," offered Davis, "as an honorably retired pastor, I do not have to attend the meetings, but, out of the goodness of my heart, I will sacrifice my time and go with you so that you don't get lost."

"Are you some kind of frickin' martyr, or am I buying when we stop for a beer on the way home?"

Davis turned to Shelly. "Can't put much over on this guy, can you?"

Chapter Ten

Boys' Day at Camp

Davis pulled into the parking lot at the St. Andrew's Presbyterian Church. He had told Jerry Ferguson that he would pick him up at one-thirty in order to drive north to Camp Kirkmont and the October meeting of the Presbytery. He pulled into an open space near the church's main entrance. Jerry and Shelly's compact blue sedan was parked in an adjacent slot.

St. Andrew's has an impressive facility, but more impressive is the commitment of the leadership to making a difference in the larger community. When they began to seek a new pastor, they were inundated with applications. From Davis' point of view, the selection of Martin and Ferguson was a double win. The church received a competent pair and the couple had a rare opportunity to work as co-pastors. As he walked through the door, he felt a bit self-conscious. The pristine décor looked like it would require an obligatory coat and tie rather than the tee-shirt and jeans he was sporting. "Oh well," he thought, "I am on my way to camp. Besides, Jerry will lighten-up this place and Shelly will maintain the class."

He followed the directional signs to a glass door that opened to the church office. Davis entered. A neatly dressed woman looked up from her keyboard. "May I help you?"

"I'm meeting Jerry to go to Presbytery."

"Of course, you must be Dr. McGowan." She spoke so matter-of-factly that Davis could only believe that either she had not noticed his clothing or she was genuinely hospitable.

"Davis, is that you?" Shelly's voice came from one of the offices beyond the secretarial area. "Come on back."

The secretary returned to her work as Davis moved toward the door to the inner office. By the time he reached it, Martin had moved out from behind her desk to greet him.

"Thanks for going with Jerry today. Being new to the area, well, you and Beth have become good friends to us."

"We feel the same."

"There's something I want to show you." She went behind her desk and pulled a photograph from the center drawer. "Just so you don't think I'm crazy."

She handed the photo to Davis. It was a group of

about fifteen people. They were wearing straw hats and leis. Two of the men were wearing grass hula skirts with coconuts strategically located over their Hawaiian shirts.

"This was our Winter Luau at the Elkhorn Church. It's an annual affair during which we snubbed the South Dakota winter. Believe me, it's quite a snub. That's me in the center. To my right is Rad Finch. The young man on the end is Ronnie. You met him at the desk of the Bendy Ditch Hotel."

Davis studied the picture. He did not know most of the people, but after pointing out Rad Finch, the likeness was obvious. "I never doubted that you were telling the truth," he said.

"I know," she said, "but I almost doubted myself. I have this picture and some others that I'm pulling together. They will be in this drawer." She pointed back to her desk. "I am also making a list of people who I knew from the Institute. In fact, I am keeping two lists. That phone call from Marlene, if that's who it was, is making me a bit paranoid."

"I understand. Who wouldn't be a bit spooked by this whole situation?"

Davis began to look around the tidy office. The bookshelves were neatly arranged in sections that he could identify. Reference books were in one area, theology in another, preaching and pastoral care in a third. In the open spaces were personal knickknacks and memorabilia.

"I can tell you do children's sermons," he said.

"How so?" she asked.

"Because you have all the teaching props." He picked up a small ram's horn that was lying on a shelf. "You have a shofar, facsimile Roman coins, and if I guess correctly, the pottery vase contains the Dead Sea Scrolls."

"Yes, Mr. Holmes, your deduction is impeccable and I confess that I am guilty of having a museum of fake curiosities."

"And if you will play Watkins to my Holmes," said Davis, "how do you understand the case at hand?"

"They were a tight group and now they are spread throughout corporate America. They don't want any witnesses, me for instance, or anyone who can put them all together. The way Jerry would say it is 'They want it to look like they met in the marketplace, when they really worked things out in the executive bathroom.'"

"Your husband does have a way with words! Okay, I'm with you. So they plot about these parachute deals which guarantee that, even if they fail, they go away rich. Then they sit on each other's boards of directors and all sing the same song: 'If we don't make these parachute deals, we won't get quality leadership.'"

"That's about as far as I can follow the trail, too," said Shelly. "But then I get stuck. I can't figure out why they are all such failures! These are not stupid people."

"There's a cultural line here somewhere."

"What do you mean, Davis?"

"I mean, that when you see bright people consistently doing something stupid, it's best to assume that they are looking at the whole thing from another point of view. If we saw it from their perspective, it would all make complete sense."

"Well, it appears that they are all getting rich at stockholder expense. That's one thing," said Martin.

"But they would be rich and respected by having a good job performance rating. As it is, they look like narcissistic incompetents, that's a hell of a price to pay. I wish I knew what they believed."

"What do you mean?"

Davis hesitated. "I don't mean 'belief' in the church sense, but their vision of what the world should look like. Osama bin Laden wants to bankrupt the western world so that we'll allow his idea of an Islamic society to be undisturbed. I doubt that these people are working for him, but the result seems about the same. Companies go down the tubes and they pay out bonuses to their friends. They redecorate their offices to the tune of millions while the company dividends are being cut. They lose market share, and get rich for being fired. Embezzle the company or run a Ponzi scheme and you go to jail. Get declared a useless bungler, and they make you rich. The result is that it's everything bin Laden could ask for."

"That can't be right, Davis. These people think they are the champions of the free enterprise system."

"Then what are they afraid of? Can you tell me that, Shelly?"

"If this was the cold war era, I'd say communism which, to them, meant the redistribution of wealth. On a positive note, they always wanted people to have a share in the economy. They really wanted the privatization of Social Security."

"Fat lot of good that would be now!"

"Well, McGowan, are you ready to hit the road?" Davis turned around to see Jerry dressed in full cowboy, Stetson to boots.

He turned to Shelly, "You meet all sorts of kids at camp!"

She laughed. "You two have fun! And don't get in trouble."

"I'm all for the fun part," offered Davis, "how 'bout you, Jerry!"

"I might even be up for some of that trouble!"

** ** **

"Exactly where are we headed?" asked Jerry as they exited Interstate 70 onto Route 4 North.

"The camp is located near a little crossroads called Zanesfield," answered McGowan.

"Near?" questioned Jerry. "In other words, it's like every other church camp I've seen. You drive about ten miles beyond nowhere and then you go a little further and you are there."

"That's about it. Of course, we minister-types have a long tradition of seeking out the nowhere places. After all, Moses met God in the wilderness; why shouldn't we?"

"Tell me about it," said Ferguson. "Shelly and I went to the wilderness and found each other."

"I know that you were both married before and lost spouses, but that's about it."

Jerry went quiet for a brief time. He scanned the rolling countryside along the highway between Dayton and Springfield. Davis had the feeling that he was seeing none of it.

"If you haven't already noticed, Shelly Martin is something else," he began. "She's strong, and not afraid of anything. Well, maybe she's afraid of some things, but not of the worst thing, being alone."

Davis was moving into his pastoral listening mood. Ferguson continued.

"She lost both her parents in a car crash when

she was a freshman in college. Not only that, they were driving up to the campus to visit her on homecoming weekend when it happened. Talk about guilt-potential. This eighteen year old kid had every reason to be bitter."

"If she ever was, she sure doesn't show it now," said Davis.

"I didn't know her then, of course, but when she has talked about it, there's no trace of bitterness in her voice. You know how tragedy makes some people angry and some people more kind and sensitive?" Davis nodded, thinking of his own past. "Well, I think Shelly became a loner for awhile, but when she came out of the wilderness, she had focus. She'd spend Saturdays at a retirement center near campus and she befriended the old ones who had no family members to visit. I think they became her family. She said it was her way of seeing her parents in later years. It gave some sort of closure on two lives that had been prematurely cut short.

"It wasn't a far leap to becoming a chaplain and thinking about a seminary education. That's when she went to the campus minister and he steered her toward becoming a ministerial candidate. Academically, she carried the day. Then again, what else did she have? Most students were just camped out in their dormitory, but for her, it was her only home."

"Sounds like a tough road," said McGowan.

"Not to hear her tell of it. When she graduated, the people from Elkhorn knew about her and pulled out all the stops. She was like all the rest of us in the sense that we thought all towns and churches were alike, usually like the one where we grew up. Anyway, they were like the family she had lost. In a lot of ways, it was an insular existence. You've seen the town. Bright people with a high standard of living, she moved in and loved them all. Met a local fellow, who she then married, and could have stayed there forever."

"*Forever* is the problem," added Davis.

"Yes. One thing you learn early in the ministry is that forever is not really an option for us breathers."

"What happened to her husband?"

"Alzheimer's hit him in his early forties and he lived into his fifties."

"Is that when your wife was sick?"

"Yes, but she had breast cancer. At least we had a life together when she was in remission."

By now they were approaching Urbana and exited the divided highway to continue north on Route 68. They drove around the monument at the center of the city, and past the little airport on the north end of town. They were cruising along farm country when Ferguson noticed a sign advertising ostrich meat. "You sure farm different livestock around here," he said.

Davis laughed. "Ohio is full of surprises, and it's not just the llamas and ostriches, either. Over in Muskingum County they have a wildlife preserve with elephants and rhinos."

"Okay, I'll take your word on that. But, did you know that there are no elk around Elkhorn?"

"I didn't know that; why the name, then?"

"I should have said, 'no elk *anymore!*' They were all eaten or trophied early on in the history of South Dakota. We do have beef though. Bet that beats ostrich."

"Careful what you say, ostrich might be on the menu at the Presbytery meeting."

After passing through West Liberty they turned on to a washboard disguised as a county road. They headed west across a valley floor. To the right was a ridge of hills.

"You call those mountains?" asked Jerry.

"No, I don't," bantered Davis, "but some people around here call them ski slopes. Put some snow on them and it's the best we can offer." The two enjoyed the ride and the openness that passed between them as friendship. They turned right at the general store in Zanesfield and started up one of the hills. The camp was at the very peak.

"I told you that I don't come to these meetings much any more," apologized Davis. "The truth is that I'm a little out of touch with what goes on in congregations. I retired early because I took a cut in pay to go to the university. Between my pension and my new salary, it was about the same, but I got some weird vibes when I announced what I was doing."

"Weird? How many pastors get asked to teach at a university? I'd say it was quite a coup."

"I thought so," said Davis. "I always enjoyed teaching in the parish, and now I would have more than a thousand students a year, some of them are even intellectually curious. In the churches I served, I had fewer than a dozen in that age group. But some people acted like I had lost my vision of ministry and was abandoning my call."

"I'd guess it was mostly jealousy," said Jerry.

"When I told the former presbytery executive, his comment was, 'You're not qualified to teach! Now, I have a master's degree and have been in academe.'"

"What an ass!" chimed in Ferguson. "What did you say to that?"

"What could I say? I just said that I had been teaching as an adjunct for a while and the university had no problems with me. After that, I just kept a low profile. So if I don't get the friendliest of welcomes, it's because some think me a quitter."

** ** **

Davis had underestimated the reaction of his colleagues who welcomed him gladly. They also welcomed the tall stranger in the cowboy hat. At dinner, the table was roaring with Jerry's tales of the Wild West, more precisely, his humorous insight into being a small town pastor in cattle country. To his relief, ham loaf, not ostrich, was on the menu.

Presbytery is the name of the regional organization for Presbyterian congregations. Representatives of churches, along with pastors, gather to discuss and implement programs of mutual concern. The camp program was a part of that emphasis, providing retreat facilities for people of all ages. Though out of the way as a meeting place, the annual trek to Zanesfield was a good excuse to meet in a place surrounded by the reds and yellows of the fall maples and birches.

During a break, Ed Hawkins cornered Davis for a private conversation.

"Are you sorry that you retired early?" asked Hawkins.

"Not at all, why?"

"Because of what's going on in the market! I'll be sixty-five next year and had planned to retire, but now I'm a little scared."

"I was, too," said Davis. "It's hard to pull the trigger and sign off on the pension, but then, again,

I'm not fully retired. I'm still saving in a 403(b) retirement account."

"Saving or losing?"

"Touché," he sighed. All the money that he had saved against the day when he could fully retire had lost value. The portfolio was now worth less than he had actually saved. "Then again, if the market was as bleak back then as it is today, I might have had third or fourth thoughts, not just second ones!" he added.

"I'd love to travel," said Ed. "Imagine being able to spend Christmas with your children and grandchildren!"

Davis completely understood. The big holidays, like weekends, were always tied to workdays for pastors. If your family lived more than a few hours away by car, a phone call had to substitute for a hug and a kiss. "Well, we're actually very lucky, Ed. We may not get paid a ton of money, but we do have a defined pension plan. Most people don't these days. And maybe even that plan will dry up, but while you are working extra years to add to your security, your grandchildren are going to outgrow sitting on your lap for a story."

"When they set up social security, what was the life expectancy, sixty-six?" asked Ed.

"Something like that," agreed Davis.

"They wanted people to retire with an average of

one year to go! Maybe that's what all this is coming to now," Hawkins added.

"You might be right, Ed. I'll say this though, my father and my father-in-law both retired early. They're in their nineties now, and I have never heard them say that they were sorry that they'd done it. That helped me decide."

"Guess I'll just have to hold my breath and sign on the dotted line."

"That's your call," said Davis. "Hey, Jerry," he added, calling across the room. "Tell Ed what you have to do when it's time to suck in your gut and do what ya gotta do!"

"Cowboy up!" came the reply.

"There," said Davis, "we've just pissed off every radical feminist in the room!"

Chapter Eleven

The Ride Home

It was pitch black before the two were back on the winding road between the camp and West Liberty. Davis felt invigorated by the renewal of relationships, and Jerry, the consummate extrovert, was riding high.

"That's a great group of people," he declared. "I can't get over how close everything is around here. In the Dakotas I might have to drive six hours to meet with that many other ministers."

"I guess that would be a big difference. When I was involved in the General Assembly of the church, we used to have all sorts of statistics. For instance, there was some high percentage, sixty to eighty percent maybe, of Presbyterians who live within five hundred miles of Pittsburgh. Of course, all the people from the Rockies gave the summary as: 'Presbyterians are more dense around Pittsburgh.'"

"I've heard that. Of course, since I went to McCormick Seminary, we thought the same about you guys who went to Princeton."

"Ouch," said Davis. "So you went to school in Chicago, and weren't really very far from Shelly."

"She was up in Evanston about the time that I was in the City, but it's a huge area, and we've tried to draw lines to see how closely our paths crossed during those years."

"It must have been a culture-shock to go out to the Dakotas after living in Chicago for three years."

"It was no problem at all," Jerry interjected. "I'm a PK, a preacher's kid, and we moved around a lot growing up. Dad served mostly in small towns. Like Shelly, I felt like I was going home when I went to my first congregation."

"Is your father still around?"

"He's in an assisted living center. Mom died fifteen years ago, and he kept right on going in the pulpit. He'd still be preaching, but his mind plays tricks on him. Sometimes he thinks it's the nineteen-fifties, and sometimes, he's in the here and now."

"Senile dementia, then?"

"Yes. Actually, that's one of the benefits of moving to Dayton. The facility where he lives is near my sister in Indianapolis. It's only two hours away."

"My daughter and her husband live in Indy," said Davis. "It's not far, but we don't get there often enough. How about you? Does your Dad know you when you're there?"

"I don't worry about that as much as I used to.

When he doesn't remember me, well, I still remember him... Shelly taught me that."

"I guess she would know."

As they talked, Jerry's cell phone came alive with several bars of music. He flipped it open to stop the sound. "I have a message from Shelly," he said. "I guess we were out of sight of cell towers back among the hills." He pushed a few buttons to play the voice message. Davis could make out the message from the driver's seat.

"I just got a call from Randy Hollows. His mother has been taken to the hospital. Apparently, she had a stroke. I'm going straight there, so don't expect me until I find out what's going on."

"That's a moment of déjà vu," said Jerry. "Bessie Hollows had a stroke a month ago."

"They often follow one another in succession," added Davis. "But maybe I should take a rain check on that beer you promised me."

"Should have known that you wouldn't forget that, McGowan! If it's all right, let's skip tonight. I should get home and see what's going on." With that, Jerry rang up Shelly's phone but it went straight to voice mail. "She's probably at the hospital," he said, "and turned her phone off."

The bright stars lost some of their nearness as they approached the city. Davis took Ferguson back to his house. His car was in the drive, but the one that Shelly had driven them both to work in was gone.

"She's not back yet," he said, "there's nothing for it, but to wait. It's too late to call the hospital, but I'll keep trying her cell phone." With that, he and McGowan said goodnight.

Davis went a block out of the way to drive past the church. He could see lights in the office, and Shelly's car parked outside. She would be home soon, he thought. "Shelly, you can't save the world–go home!" he said aloud, and then added, "and turn on your cell phone!"

Chapter Twelve

The Morning After

McGowan reached for the phone. He thought he had gotten it on the second ring, but the truth was it was five-thirty in the morning and it might have been ringing for half an hour.

"McGowan's." In his half-numb mind Davis tried to remember who was in the hospital, and then he remembered that was a previous life. He didn't make hospital calls anymore. At eight o'clock in the morning, he would be standing in front of forty students in Religion 204.

"Davis, she didn't come home last night. Something is wrong."

"Jerry? That's impossible. I drove by the church last night and she was there."

"That's where I am now. She's not here. Her car is outside and the lights are on in her office, but there's nothing, no note, nothing."

"Have you called the police?" asked Davis.

"They're here right now, but they're just asking dumb questions. They are asking about her mood, when I last saw her, and did we have a fight? They don't seem to believe a word of it. I thought that maybe you could tell them…"

"Jerry, calm down. Ask them if it would help if I came down right now. I could be there in fifteen minutes." The phone went silent for a moment, then Jerry came back.

"Yes, that would help!"

"Did you call the hospital about that stroke patient? Maybe she's there."

"I went down there myself. I thought that maybe she had ridden down with someone from the family. But, Davis, Bessie was not even brought into the hospital. She hasn't been there since she was discharged last month. They think I'm talking nonsense."

"Did you play them the message on your cell phone?"

"Yes, and all they did was confiscate the phone."

"Hold on, Jerry, I'll be right there."

By now, Beth was wide awake and listening to the conversation. "What happened?" she asked.

"Evidently Shelly did not come home last night. Jerry is beside himself and the cops are asking for information when he thinks they should be jumping into action." He pulled on his clothes and gave Beth a quick kiss. "I'll probably have to go straight to campus, if I even make it to class." Beth may have called to him, but he didn't hear as he hurried out to the garage.

The trip from Fairborn to Beavercreek is quicker at five-thirty in the morning than during mall hours or between classes at WSU. He arrived at St. Andrew's Church in less than the promised fifteen minutes. Jerry was seated with his head buried in his hands as Davis came through the door. Jerry jumped to his feet, but a uniformed police officer stepped between them.

"Are you Dr. McGowan?" asked the man. The shiny silver name plate on his crisp shirt said "Collins."

"Yes," said Davis, "Jerry called…"

"I would like you to come with me into the next room. I need to ask you a few questions." He led Davis into Shelly's office and closed the door. "Rev. Ferguson says that you were with him the last time he saw his wife. Is that right?"

"Yes, we were in this room. I had come to pick up Jerry. We were going to a meeting up near Zanesfield. Shelly wanted to show me a picture."

"Rev. Ferguson said that you were going to Zanesville."

"They are new to the area; I'm sure he was confused. He probably remembered the 'Zanes' part. We were going to Camp Kirkmont near West Liberty."

The man nodded. "The picture she was showing you, is it here?"

"It was in the center drawer of her desk."

"Can you show me?"

Davis hesitated, "Don't you need to protect the area for fingerprints?"

"I'll bet you watch a lot of TV, Doc. This is a public office; it's full of fingerprints. Now, you show me something interesting and I'll tell you not to touch."

McGowan was set back by the change in tone, but said nothing. He walked around the desk to where he could open the center drawer. "The picture was in here," he said opening the drawer. "Shelly made a point of showing me where it was." Through the increasing opening he could see a neatly arranged tray with paper clips, rubber bands, and disposable pens. The corner where she had set the photo was empty. The only thing else in the drawer was a rolled up piece of paper. "It's not here," he said, reaching for the rolled paper.

"What's that?" asked the officer.

"Isaiah," said McGowan.

"It's a miniature scroll, a small copy of the Isaiah scroll. It's a tourist item. She has a lot of those sorts of things in the office. They're great props for junior sermons and teaching classes."

"Is there anything else missing, other than the picture?"

"I was only here for a few minutes, but everything looks the same. I picked up that shofar over there," he pointed to the ram's horn. The Roman coins and pottery jar were also still there. "Everything seems the same."

"Why did she show you the picture?"

"That's hard to explain. Shelly used to live in a small town in South Dakota. When she and Jerry moved to Dayton, she found that some of the people she knew in the Dakotas were here in town. The problem was that when she bumped into them, they all acted like they didn't know her."

"Maybe they just didn't recall her."

"No, I was there when she talked to them. They were very abrupt. They didn't act like she was some stranger and this was just an innocent case of mistaken identity. Anyway, it was important to her that she showed me that this rejection wasn't a little thing. These people had been close friends; they would not have forgotten her."

"Were you having an affair with her?"

Davis bolted back. "No! I have only known her for a couple of months. My wife and I invited them to the symphony. The four of us are becoming friends. She wanted me to know that she was being completely truthful. That's all!"

"Sorry, Dr. McGowan, but I have to ask these things. How would a picture prove anything?"

"Well, I personally know one of the people who shunned her when the four of us were at the Schuster. The picture that she showed me was taken years ago at a church social party– back in South Dakota. It was very clear that the people who I had seen blowing her off at the Philharmonic used to be close friends."

"Who were they?"

"The one I knew was Rad Finch." Davis looked for the cop to react, but his body language didn't show anything. "There was also a young man named Ronnie that I had met once, and a woman named Marlene Zeller." Officer Collins did a double-take at the mention of Zeller.

"What do you know of her?"

"Nothing, except what Shelly has told me. Marlene was a member of Shelly's church in South Dakota. Shelly felt she knew her well, and had helped her through the loss of her mother."

"How long were you with Rev. Ferguson yesterday?"

"Well, I picked him up here around one-thirty. We left together, and, as I said, we went up north to a meeting that went through dinner. On the way home, he got a voice message on his cell phone. It was Shelly saying that she was going to the hospital; a church member was taken in for an apparent stroke..."

"Did you actually hear the message?"

"Yes, it was pretty loud and I could make out what was being said. Anyway, when we got back to town, I dropped him off at his house between ten and ten-thirty. After leaving him there, I drove by the church here and saw Shelly's car and the lights on in the church. I figured she would be back home soon."

"Did you stop at the church?"

"No, it was already late and I wanted to get home, too. I'm supposed to teach an eight o'clock class this morning."

Collins looked at his watch. "Where do you teach?"

"Just down the road at Wright State."

"Well, you'll probably make it. I'm just about done with questions."

"What about Jerry?"

"He's reported a missing person. In this kind of domestic case, we usually like to take a good look at the spouse. You've backed up everything he said earlier, so it looks like, for now, we have to hope that his wife will turn up somewhere, and that she's fine."

"How likely is that?" asked Davis.

Collins just shook his head. "I don't see a simple family fight that got out of control." The two were moving out of the office toward the secretarial work area. Once they were outside the room, Collins stopped. "I have to ask you one more thing, Dr. McGowan. Did you know that the room we were just in is being monitored?" It was Davis' turn to be shocked.

"No, I..."

"It probably was yesterday, too. I'm just a city cop, so I get underestimated most of the time. But around here, most of us have military training and can spot a bug. Before we tip off whoever is watching, we'll bring in someone who can follow it back to its source. Someone knows what happened in there, and you seem to be the only one who knows that something is now missing."

The last statement did not ease Davis' mind. He did not want to be linked to anything other than a lecture that was to begin in forty-five minutes. On the other hand, his troubles seemed slight when compared to what Jerry was going to face. He looked around for his friend. His eyes found him sitting in the hall beyond the glass walls of the outer office. It looked like someone was with him. Davis went out to him.

"Davis, this is Ginny Schaeffer, our business manager; she came in as soon as she heard."

"Thanks for coming," said McGowan. Turning to Ferguson he said, "Jerry, I have to go to campus for a class, but I will be back in an hour. Promise me that you'll wait."

"Where else can I go?"

Chapter Thirteen

Message from Shelly

McGowan had thrown his briefcase in the back seat of the car, an indication that he was thinking more clearly at five-thirty in the morning than he was now as he raced to his eight o'clock class. He swiped his faculty ID to enter the gated parking area near Allyn Hall. After a brisk walk which included two flights of stairs, he was soon standing at the head of the class. Most students were drinking cola or coffee to try to shake off the early morning fuzzies.

"They probably won't even notice the stubble or the jeans," thought Davis. They did, however, notice that there was no handout or writing assignment to take back to the dorm. The hour was spent doing what Davis did best, adlibbing an entertaining lecture that had a foundation in scholarship.

It was his best gift. He had the ability to pull ideas together, sometimes on the spur of the moment. A former colleague from his years as a pastor put him on the spot once by asking a waitress to guess what McGowan did for a living.

The group seated around the table had been laughing, and the banter spilled over to the server who was also quick on the uptake. It was then that the question was posed: "Can you guess what he does for a living?"

The server thought and then surrendered without a try. "I don't know," she said, "what?"

McGowan looked her in the eye and said with a straight face, "They pay me to talk!"

He was in a whole new career now, but he was still being paid to talk. At the end of the class a student in the front row asked, "Did you have a rough night last night, Dr. McGowan? Looks like you haven't been home."

"Ah, pulled an all-nighter writing a term paper," he quipped, "but thank you for noticing."

The trick now was to get into his office without running into anyone who would know that he was coming from class. He climbed the steps to the third floor and used his key to enter the back hallway to the office suite. The corridor was deserted, so he had no problem escaping the scrutiny of a critical eye. Then again, the department was pretty forgiving, more so than some congregations that he had served.

Davis logged onto his desktop computer. He would check his messages and tell the department's

Administrative Specialist that he would be away from his office, but back in time for his philosophy class at one-forty. He picked up the phone to call her station in the main office.

"Erin," he said when she answered, "this is Davis. Something has come up, and I am going to cancel my office hours this morning."

"Does it have anything to do with that friend of yours who disappeared?"

"What?"

"It's on the news. I think they are planning a press conference at ten o'clock."

"Actually, it does have something to do with that; I'm surprised that the word is out so soon." He hung up the phone, and keyed in the password of his email account. New message tags scrolled down the screen. Most were labeled "announcements" on the faculty listserv, but there was one that was not tied to a campus address. It was from Shelly Martin.

Davis stared for a moment. It had been received at nine-forty the night before. That is when he and Jerry had set out from Kirkmont on the way home. He clicked to open the message:

> Hello, Davis-
> The women's study-group cleared out twenty minutes ago and I have been try-
> ing to get down some of my thoughts

about the empty boxes. Obviously, that was part of their inside communication. We've all said that it's important to 'think outside the box' but I stopped using that phrase in Elkhorn because it always drew a snigger. They obviously had something else in mind so I have strained my databanks and these are the things I remember about boxes:

- Value is not contained in a box
- Value does not disappear, it moves
- People buy boxes
- Value moves in transactions, not boxes
- Selling the box preserves the value
- Boxes gain value based on what people think they're worth

That's I all I can remember now, but I'll keep thinking. BTW, Rad Finch called me a few minutes ago to apologize about what happened at the Schuster. Go figure!

"And how the hell did he know to call you at your office at nine o'clock at night?" thought Davis.

He hit the print button on the screen. He no longer cared who saw him; this was too important.

To retrieve the message he had to go to the file room where the departmental printer was located. That meant passing through the main reception area where Erin was stationed.

"Davis, you look hung-over," she declared as he rounded the corner and entered the reception area.

"Come on, I can't look that bad!" he protested.

"It's just that you are usually neatly dressed. I take it that you have been involved with whatever is going on. What do you know?"

"Not much, I was with Jerry Ferguson last night. That's Shelly's husband. She wasn't home when we got back and apparently never came home. He's a basket case. We all are! Excuse me, but I have to get going."

He grabbed the copy from the bin in the printer. There were two pages. He looked at them figuring that someone else had a print job in the same queue, but there were two copies of the same email. "I must have double-clicked," he thought.

He returned to his office to grab his jacket. He folded one email up and stuck it in the liner pocket of the coat. The other he placed in a file drawer out of sight.

Stairs are generally faster than elevators, and Davis was down them and out the door heading for the car. He now had something real to show that Shelly was in her office while he and Jerry were on the way home. As that idea crossed his mind, it collided with a second: "Why or how did Ferguson get the phone message saying that she was on her way to the hospital?"

Chapter Fourteen

The Paparazzi

As Davis approached the St. Andrew's Church, he could see that the parking lot was full. At least four vans with satellite antennae mounted on top were in position. The major networks were fully represented in the reporters and camera crews already assembled. This was a press conference, not the paparazzi, yet McGowan knew that the effect on a traumatized Jerry Ferguson would be the same. He stood by his car for a time trying to identify a familiar face. As he looked into the crowd, someone approached from the left.

"Dr. McGowan?" It was Collins, the police officer that had interviewed him earlier.

"Isn't this overkill for the first hours of a missing person's report?" asked Davis.

"I told you that this case doesn't seem to fit the normal domestic disturbance scenario. It may be helpful to put people on the lookout earlier."

"You did say that, Officer Collins. I just feel for Jerry, this is just so over the top."

"Dr. McGowan, this is Agent John Smith from the FBI. He wants to talk to you."

Davis turned to the man who had stepped up beside the policeman. He had on a black ball cap, a khaki jacket and loose fitting jeans. McGowan thought about saying, "I thought you guys always wore black suits," but he had already been accused of watching too much TV earlier. Instead, he said something even dumber. "John Smith?"

"If you prefer, it can be 'Doe,' 'Jones,' 'Johnson,' or 'Abedinejad.' The point is that you won't know my name; it's not important."

"Sorry," said McGowan.

"Don't be," said the agent. "You got the point right away; I think we'll be able to talk straight to one another, but not here. How about you take me for a ride in your car? We need to talk, but off the record for now."

It seemed like a setup in a bad movie. Davis looked to Collins. "It's okay," said the cop.

"I can show you my badge, but it might cause a scene," said Smith or Jones or Abedinejad. Davis opened his driver-side car door and hit the button to unlock the passenger door. Smith got in beside him. "Take a right out of the parking lot," he instructed Davis.

They drove for a quarter mile before the agent spoke again. "Take a right on Indian

Ripple Road," he said. "Not far ahead on the right is a park called The Narrows. Pull in there and we'll talk."

Davis knew the place. It was a small nature reserve where school children on school outings could see maple trees tapped for syrup. He slowed down at the yellow road sign announcing a park entrance ahead. He pulled into a space at the far end of the lot, but was relieved to see that there were other cars and people walking about.

When he killed the engine, Smith began to talk.

"Sorry about all this cloak and dagger stuff, Davis– May I call you Davis?" He'd asked the question, but didn't wait for an answer. "I'm here because of something you said to Brian Collins this morning." Davis noted that Officer Collins actually had a first name which, unlike Smith's, was probably real. "You told him that this Shelly Martin had told you that she received a call from Marlene Zeller."

"She *thought* that it was Marlene," corrected Davis. "The caller didn't identify herself, but Shelly recognized the voice."

"How well did she know Zeller?"

"Apparently they were very close at one time, but that was when they lived in the same small town in South Dakota."

"Elkhorn, right?" said Smith.

McGowan wondered how much the agent knew since he was already jumping ahead to fill in the blanks of Davis' story. "Yes, in Elkhorn. Shelly was the pastor in that town for eleven years. During that time, a number of people took up residence there to work at or attend the Elkhorn Institute. She knew them all, but they acted like they hadn't ever met her when we ran into some of them at the symphony last month."

"Did she offer you any proof that she really knew these people?"

"She had a photograph. In fact, she called me into her office yesterday to show it to me. She pointed out the few people I knew in the picture."

"And they were?"

"Shelly herself, Marlene Zeller, Rad Finch, and a young man named Ronnie, who works at the hotel."

"That would be Ronnie Wilkins."

Davis turned abruptly in his seat. "How did...," he began, but Smith talked through the gasp.

"Did she point me out?"

David was stunned to a shocked silence.

"Of course, she didn't," continued the agent. "She only pointed to the people she thought you might be able to identify."

Davis chose his next words very carefully. "So you know Shelly? You know all these people. Why are you baiting me?"

"Yes, I lived in Elkhorn," said Smith, "but I'm not baiting you. Right now, I am leveling with you. I already know what I know. I need to determine what you know. Shelly was one of my favorite people. You knew her; I'm sure you understand that."

"What I don't understand is why you are suddenly using the past tense in talking about her!"

"Sorry, I meant nothing by it. Elkhorn is in the past, so Shelly is there in my mind– in the past, that is."

His words seemed to fit, but Davis had no balance to weigh them against. As he was pondering whether this stranger was trustworthy, Agent Smith spoke again. This time his words were almost inaudible.

"People who disappear like this usually don't come back."

That sentence took away all the air in the car. Davis cracked the window and a cool draught drenched his face and awakened his senses. "Poor Jerry," he said, "what will happen to him?"

"For a while he'll be very busy. There will be teams out searching, and he will keep telling himself that she's going to walk through the door and give him a kiss on the cheek."

"Will they find her?" asked Davis

A shrug of the shoulders and then, "They found Marlene Zeller this morning. Apparently, it was a suicide, an overdose of pills. There was a note."

"Not a good time to be from Elkhorn, is it?" said McGowan. This time, the FBI agent was silent.

"Here's something that you don't know," started McGowan. "I didn't tell Collins because it just happened when I went to campus for my class."

"What's that?"

"Shelly sent me an email last night. It was sent about the time Jerry and I were leaving our meeting." He reached into his jacket pocket to retrieve the folded paper. "I printed it out."

Smith took the paper and opened it. He read through Shelly's list of statements. "They sure underestimated that lady," he said. There was no malice in his tone. "They liked her because she was like everyone's sister or mother.

They figured that all their ideology would blow past her at the speed of light. But, she was listening, wasn't she?"

"Seems that way," agreed Davis. "What do you make of the fact that Finch called her that same evening?"

"You're good, McGowan! I'm the agent and you are deposing me!" He was correct. There were moments in the encounter when John Smith, or whatever his name was, had lost his professional distance. Then again, how could Davis be sure of anything?

"What do you think about Finch's call?" Smith had turned the question around.

"Could have been a number of things," Davis said. "He might have been trying to find out where she was. He might have just been apologizing. But there's something else that doesn't make any sense whatsoever. If Shelly was in her office, writing a note to me, and getting a call from Rad Finch, why did she call Jerry to say that she had been called out to the hospital?"

"Did she go to the hospital?"

"Apparently not since the woman she was supposed to see there was at home all the time."

"Then I'd say that someone was trying to

frame your friend Jerry."

"Huh? By giving him a voice message as evidence to provide an alibi? I don't get it."

"I've already told you more than you're allowed to know. You're the philosopher. You've studied logic. Figure it out. Anything can be made to look like something else. They teach that at Elkhorn. Your friend is going to need your cool head."

Chapter Fifteen

Remedy for Fear

Agent Smith got out of the car while the two were still parked at The Narrows. Davis questioned whether it would be better if he took him back to the church. Smith just smiled, and raised his arm in a gesture of greeting. An engine started at the other end of the parking lot and back-up lights flared as the engine was set in reverse. "Oh," thought McGowan, "I have to learn to think differently. I'm in another world now."

When he pulled back into the parking lot at the church, the media vans and cameras had disappeared, but the activity had not subsided. In the center of the action was Jerry Ferguson. He was making his way through the crowd with pictures of Shelly that had been made on the office copier. While the images had a vague resemblance to a human being, the picture quality was so poor that it gave no clue to the identity of its subject. Some of the people had

small posters with clearer images. The photo-
copies were obviously a Plan B, a last resort after the inkjet printers went dry.

"The important thing to ask is if anyone
saw her in the past twelve hours," Jerry was
repeating the instructions like a mantra as he
approached Davis. When he saw McGowan his
face lit up. "Isn't the turnout great?"

"It's quite a crowd, Jerry."

"I figure that we will be able to cover every
house in a four-block radius by dinner. We
have other crews going to businesses to put up
signs. I figure that someone had to see her."

"I'm sure you're right," agreed McGowan.
His words belied what he was really feeling.
He found himself thinking about the advice he
used to give to parents during the Cold War. It
was odd, he thought, that all the frenzied activity around disseminating information about
Shelly's disappearance felt like the ploy rec-
ommended by child psychologists. In those
days, children would have nightmares about
nuclear holocaust, and parents were unsure as
to how to reassure them. "Action is the remedy
for fear" was a common theme. Get them doing
something, anything, to promote peace. Kids
drew a lot of posters with flowers and peace
signs. They wrote notes and letters to presi-

dents and premiers telling them to destroy the weapons, not the people. Of course, none of that made any more sense than "duck and cover" in the fifties when McGowan and Mrs. Perkins' other third graders would crawl under their desks at Sheridan Elementary School. That, too, was to protect them from all the harms that humanity could deal out.

Now Davis was looking at Jerry, a man who desperately wanted to believe in the power of children's art and the safety of a plywood desk. "This is really quite something," he said. "Have you had anything to eat today?" Of course, he hadn't; neither had Davis for that matter. "We need to sit down, and get some food; otherwise, we'll not be able to sustain the search."

The last words must have struck a chord, because it stopped his frenetic activity. "I'll tell Ginny that we are going to get something to eat," he said. Davis understood him to mean Ginny Schaeffer, the church's business manager whom he had met earlier that morning.

"I'll tell her," replied Davis. He had seen Ginny sitting at a table where people were signing up for neighborhood routes. "For all the ridicule church people take from the public, they can organize and are goodhearted," thought McGowan. He walked over to where

Schaeffer was seated. "Ginny, I am going to try to get Jerry to sit down for a rest. I'm taking him to lunch."

"That's a good idea," she answered. "The Presbytery Office called; they are sending over cold cuts and bread for all the volunteers, but I think he should get away for awhile."

"Good," he agreed. "If we're still here when the food arrives, he'll be tempted to stay on through and eat with the others. See ya!"

"Thanks, Davis."

** ** **

Davis had to literally take Jerry by the arm to get him to move. He recognized the minivan driven by the presbytery executive pulling in as he was pulling out. If they had stayed another few minutes, Jerry would have opted to stay and eat with the volunteers. "There's a breakfast/brunch place right across from campus. How 'bout we get something there?"

"Sounds good!" said Ferguson, "As long as we're not away too long."

"Do you have your cell phone?" asked Davis. "They'll be able to reach you."

"But, I don't have it. Shit! The cops took it because it had Shelly's message on it."

"Don't worry," consoled Davis, "I have mine. Here, call Ginny so that she has this number." He handed over the phone.

Jerry took it and called Schaeffer's cell number. "Ginny, this is Jerry. I forgot that the police took my cell phone. I'm calling from Davis' phone, so use this number if you have to get hold of me for anything. Thanks. Oh, okay, that's good. Thank her for me! Bye."

"What was that about?" asked Davis.

"Oh, right after we left, the presbytery exec showed up with a mess of food for the volunteers. We could have eaten right there."

"Maybe it's worked out for the better, Jer. They're being taken care of, and we can have a little time to map out a longer-term strategy and put some of the pieces together." Davis feared this last part. Between his own thoughts and Agent Smith's the pieces were starting to fit together too well to allow for the growth of hope. He took the phone back from Jerry and called Erin at the University.

"Erin, this is Davis. I've never done this before, but I won't be back for my class at one-forty. It's just down the hall in 301; would you place a sign on the board?"

"I'll be glad to do that," she answered. "Are you sure you're okay?"

"I'm fine; things are just a little wild right now. Why do you ask?"

"Well, campus security came up and took your PC out of your office. I've put in for a re-placement, but thought you should know in advance."

Chapter Sixteen

Denial

When the two arrived at the restaurant, they were greeted immediately. Davis knew the hostess and asked for a booth in an area isolated from the rest of the dining area by a glass wall. In earlier times it had been the smoking section, but now that they were seated, it substituted as a sanctuary space.

Jerry was, by nature, an extrovert and his method of coping with an overwhelming situation was to jabber on about the efficiency of the police and their quick response to announce a search.

"I think it gives us some a reason to hope, don't you?" he asked.

Davis was not ready to pull the rug out from under his friend by voicing his own doubts. "It would have been a disaster if they had put everything off," he answered.

His thoughts, however, were quite the contrary. This was a disaster, period. His conversation with the alleged Agent Smith had left him very little wiggle room. He wished that he could get caught up in the adrenalin rush of the search, but instead he was sinking into a depression. He would have liked to grieve for Shelly, but he had to keep Jerry going until the last hope was doused.

Ferguson was still dealing with "where" and Davis was wandering among the "whys."

"We need to think about tonight, Jerry," he stated. "Why don't you plan to stay with us for the night?"

Ferguson was emphatic. "No can do! I want to be at the house when Shelly gets home."

"Okay, that makes sense," said Davis against the screaming voice in his brain that said, *It won't happen like that!* Instead he said, "Is there anyone that you can call to come and stay with you?"

"My sister, Grace, is coming from Indianapolis. She's going to come and stay until Shelly's back. I called her right away, and she said she'd go make sure the staff at the nursing home knew that she wouldn't be in for a few days. Did I tell you that my Dad is in a home there?"

"Yes," said Davis.

"We moved him there when he couldn't live alone anymore. It was convenient with my sister in Indy and all. She teaches there at IUPUI."

"That's enough letters to make vegetable soup!" McGowan knew the school, but was using one of the pastoral care techniques that were a part of his professional tools. When someone is in shock, invite them to talk about something "normal" from another time and place.

"Sorry," Ferguson apologized. "It's a university partnership between Purdue and Indiana Universities. 'IUPUI' is 'Indiana University / Purdue University at Indianapolis'."

"She teaches there?"

"Yes, my little sister is the brains in the family with a PhD in Anthropology."

"So she teaches Anthro?"

"Not exactly. She does studies within the hospital system. Tries to figure out the cultural barriers that keep certain groups of patients from seeking care or following treatment schedules. Sounds goofy, but it saves lives."

"What time do you think she'll get here?" asked Davis.

"She'll want to be there to help Dad eat tonight, and then close up the house. Make sure the cat has enough food and water for a few days. I'd guess she'll be here by nine o'clock or so."

The server, who had identified himself earlier as Chad, came to take the order. Davis realized that they hadn't opened the menu, but that didn't really matter.

"I'll have the blueberry pancakes with sausage," he said.

"Links or patties?"

"Links, please."

Chad turned to Ferguson. "And for you, Sir?"

"That sounds good to me, I'll have the same."

The server took the menus. "I'll have your food shortly," he added.

Davis wondered how many people had seen the morning news. If they had, no one seemed curious about Ferguson whose image highlighted the reports.

"I will really be insulted if you don't let me stay with you until your sister arrives," said Davis. Ministers are caregivers. They are used to helping others, but, like physicians and nurses, are terrible on the receiving end. Davis phrased his comment so that Jerry could not wave it off in an effort to 'cowboy up'.

"I'd like that," said Ferguson. "I have to stay at the house, but I don't really want to be there alone!"

To McGowan, the last comment sounded honest to the core.

** ** **

By five o'clock the number of volunteers had thinned, and those remaining were about at their wit's end. Reports of Shelly had come in throughout the day. She was spotted at a rest stop on I-75 near

Sidney, and as far south as Lexington, Ky. In the end, nothing checked out positive.

Ferguson kept encouraging people by maintaining a frenetic pace of moving between clusters of volunteers. Davis wondered, however, if his motivation had not shifted at some point. Earlier, he was sending groups out to search, and now, toward the end of the day, he was trying to hold them close at hand, knowing that if they left, he would be alone.

"We need to go home," said Davis. "Let's let the others close up here. We should set up shop at the house. That will be the best station for evening."

"Yes," agreed Ferguson, "that's where Shelly will come."

More than anything, McGowan did not want Jerry to feel abandoned by the day's efforts.

"Ginny, thanks," he said. "I am going to take Jerry home. If you would set the church phones so that the calls get forwarded there, that would be great! Give us fifteen minutes, and we will be properly installed for the night shift."

Ginny Schaeffer perked up. Davis took it to mean that she understood what he was trying to do. As it was, Jerry would have held on and on. Now the clock had started, and he needed to get moving to his next important duty.

For Ferguson, the next duty was to attend the phones. In Davis' opinion, his next responsibility was to get Jerry to lie down.

Jerry was anxious to get moving after McGowan's announcement. Unconsciously, the change in activity was telling his numbed senses that there was movement, and if there was movement, maybe some progress was being made.

They were not home five minutes when the food began to arrive. Davis had guessed that food for dinner would not be a problem. The problem was storage. At the same time, Ferguson's behavior started to change.

"Did I ever show you my Peacemaker?" he asked.

"No," said Davis, who had never been inside the house. He followed him back to the den where there were two desks facing opposite walls. Jerry opened a drawer in an oak credenza and pulled out a shiny mahogany case. Opening the lid, he revealed a silver revolver on a bed of red velvet.

"It's only a replica," he said. "It's an 1873 Single Action Army Colt .45."

"Yep, Jer, you are a cowboy!" Ferguson chuckled a little and Davis felt that maybe Jerry would be able to settle down now that he was in his own house. One by one, Ferguson brought out little treasures and memorabilia. McGowan noted that everything he explained related to a part of his life before his marriage to Shelly. Jerry was seeking comfort away from the reminders of his missing wife.

Looking around the room, Davis noted empty spaces beside each desk.

"Aren't you supposed to have computers here?" he asked.

"What?" Jerry seemed to startle. "Oh, the police took them. Said it was standard. They wanted to see who has contacted us. I told them no one, but they wanted to be safe. They also wanted to see any photos that Shelly had."

Ferguson seemed so upbeat about these disclosures, but Davis felt like screaming, "How could her photos help them? They won't know who the people are!"

Instead, he whispered, "Well, they are thorough. Guess they know what they're doing." And a part of him wanted to believe that they knew exactly what they were doing.

** ** **

When Grace arrived at nine-thirty, Jerry was asleep. Davis waved her into the kitchen where they had a cup of tea which he brewed from Shelly's stash of teabags. The two talked openly about the events of the day, and McGowan expressed his ongoing concern that Jerry was in danger of total exhaustion. The people around him needed to see that he was getting food and rest. Grace agreed.

"What do you think happened?" She asked. Davis hesitated using words that he had not yet spoken aloud.

"I think she was abducted."

"But, why?"

"I have spoken with the authorities and it's all conjecture, mind you, but we think that she knew something that might cause a lot of people trouble." Davis was skirting a great many issues. He did not offer any elaboration on what "authorities" meant and made no mention of Smith, the FBI, or Marlene Zeller.

"What could she have known that was so dangerous? Shelly is an absolute sweetheart."

"I don't think it's *what* she knew so much as *who* she knew. Grace, I am going to ask you to do something for me."

"Whatever you want, you're taking care of my big brother."

"You are going to be here awhile. Snoop around a little. I'm interested in pictures, specifically photographs of Shelly and people from her church in South Dakota. She showed me one once. It was of a church supper, a theme party, a luau. Everyone was in Hawaiian shirts, if that helps. The people in that picture were important, and it seems like it was the only thing taken out of her office. The police have taken all the pictures from here that they could find along with the computers. They even took the computer out of my office at the University when I told them I had an email from her."

"Then that's good, right?"

"I don't know. I'd like to think so, but I'd feel better if it wasn't all disappearing so rapidly. I know this sounds paranoid, but I'd like to have a copy of some of this. The people she knows are powerful, and I'm not so sure how deep that goes."

Grace took a deep breath. "This is scary; how much does my brother know?"

"At this point, nothing."

"Good. I'll look for pictures."

Chapter Seventeen

McGowan's World

The next morning, Davis awoke in his own bed. After showering and shaving, he felt like he had been reborn into the human race, and, after having a bowl of cereal with Beth, he was driving to campus. He stopped at the Hangar, the student eatery, for a cup of coffee on the way to his office. His goal for the day was to make amends for the previous day's delinquent behavior by reworking lectures for the next day's class.

His office looked the same though he knew that the computer had been switched out in the FBI's search for information about Shelly's disappearance. It seemed like wasted effort since most of the data was not held on his desktop at all. He kept all his data on the University's mainframe. The PC was merely an entry portal for the larger database. This was provided to faculty so that they could log on to their computers from any terminal in the University system.

Davis turned on the PC and poked around the

files. His score on Freecell was zero, but that was all that seemed to have changed. When he logged on his email server, however, all messages from Shelly had been deleted. "They certainly did their job," thought McGowan.

There was a knock on the door. It was Denton Barstow, the Department Chair. Before Davis could get any words out, Barstow was expressing concern.

"The news report didn't look good," he said.

Davis shook his head. "Shelly's husband is in denial, but who wouldn't be. It's too much to take in."

"They interviewed the Chief of Police who, very matter of factly, said, 'In most of these domestic cases, the spouse is the first suspect' and then he added, 'we've found no evidence of foul play.' Seemed sort of backhanded."

Davis hadn't seen the news, and didn't know how to address it. "Anyone watching Jerry yesterday would know that he wants nothing more than to have Shelly back."

"Well, it's terrible. And then they found Marlene Zeller dead from an overdose, but no one has any record of how she could have gotten the drugs. They were by prescription only, but she didn't have any record of having taken those sorts of medication."

"Did the report try to link Zeller's death with Martin's disappearance?"

"Yes and no. It wasn't so much what was said, as what wasn't. The Chief spoke to both situations at the same conference, and then opened the floor to reporters' questions. One reporter asked if the two stories were related, and he said, 'We are trying to establish if the two knew each other, but the two events seem unrelated.'"

"Well," said Davis, "they did know each other quite well, and that should be easy enough to trace. If they check the funeral home that buried Zeller's mother, they will find that Shelly Martin conducted the service."

"It sounds like you know more than the police." Denton stepped back. "Looks like there's a student here to see you. If there's anything I can do, let me know, Davis." Barstow stepped out of the office and was replaced by a student from McGowan's eight o'clock class.

"Hi," said Davis, "what can I do for you?"

"Sorry to bother you, Dr. McGowan, but I working on my term paper and I have a question about how I should make parenthetical references to the Bible."

"Okay, show me what you have."

She set her backpack down on one of the chairs and pulled out a blue report folder. She withdrew her paper and set it out on the desk for Davis to see. She was writing a paper on the Dead Sea Scrolls.

"This is an interesting topic. It's a discovery that has really changed our understanding of the Bible," observed Davis.

"I think the whole idea of all the various scrolls and how they were written and preserved is fascinating. The first day of class you told us about how they made paper and how many manuscripts we have; I never heard anything like that before! I thought that the King James Bible was it!"

"A lot of people were brought up that way," said Davis. "Let me show you how to reference the Bible. You know how you normally put the author's last name and the page number? Well, with the Bible just put the chapter and verse in the parenthesis. Then make sure that you list the particular Bible you are using on your 'Works Cited' page." They went over the paper and Davis offered suggestions.

When they had finished, the woman made a confession. "When I go home my Grandma asks me what I learn in your class, but I can't tell her. If I told her about these scrolls, for instance, she'd just tell me that I wasn't studying the 'real' Bible."

"Meaning, the King James Bible," responded Davis.

"Exactly," said the young woman.

"It's hard to let go of things that you know in order to see things differently," offered McGowan. "She's just holding on to what she learned growing up."

"She raised me, but I'm the first one from my family to go to college. I go back home and try to tell them what I learn here, and they say that I'm getting all stuck up. My sister is the worst."

"You love them, and I'd guess that they feel like they are losing you. You are learning about things they never heard of. It doesn't make you any better or worse than they are, but it does change the way you see and talk about the world. They only see that you are changing."

McGowan saw tears welling in her eyes.

"I know it hurts," he said. "The sad thing is that they should be proud of what you're doing. And yet, it scares them. Just love them, and hang in there."

When she left the room, Davis tried to take stock of where he was. He had two weeks until the term was ended. After that, he'd have six weeks between Thanksgiving and New Year's before winter term began. He had a friend he could try to stand by, but not help. One thing he could do was to tell the Chief of Police that it would be a simple thing to draw a connecting line between Shelly Martin and Marlene Zeller.

Chapter Eighteen

Monday, Monday

By Monday morning Davis had all his classes back on schedule with the syllabus. The detective handling the Marlene Zeller investigation had taken his statement about the connection between the two cases, and Grace Ferguson was collaborating on the mental state of her brother. On one visit, she pulled McGowan to one side and explained that she hadn't been able to find any photos that fit the description. "I'm afraid that Shelly was well-organized and kept all those sorts of things together," she said. "Whoever took the computers scooped up everything."

After class, he picked up a fresh coffee and walked the three flights of stairs to his office. Balancing his coffee and books in one hand, he unlocked his office door with the other. In the darkened room, he could see a red light blinking on the phone indicating that there was a message.

Turning on the light with his elbow, he set everything down on his desk, lifted the handset, and punched in his telephone pass code. The message was from Ella Sanderson, the new presbytery executive. Davis did not know this woman well. He had retired prior to her arrival, but his view of her arriving with sandwiches the week before made him confident that she was a no-nonsense, caring leader.

"Davis, thank you for returning my call," she began. "I was calling about Jerry Ferguson. Everywhere I turn, your name comes up as a friend of his. I need to ask you a big favor, that is, if you can help."

Davis was tempted to say, "Why, what's the matter?", but an automatic response wouldn't fit in this slot. Everything was the matter!

Instead, he said, "I'll do whatever I can."

"Good," she replied. "I thought that I'd try to support the people at St. Andrew's by attending services there yesterday. Jerry is trying to push his way through this by strength of will, and I'm just afraid for him."

"I know he's trying to tough this out," answered McGowan. "It's almost like he thinks that a positive attitude will bring Shelly home and if he lets down for a minute, it will be his fault."

"That's what I feel, too," said Ella. "I know you are staying close to him, but can you stand a little closer?"

"I would have been there yesterday," explained Davis, "but I had already agreed to teaching classes over at College Hill Community Church for the next three weeks."

"I'll tell you what, how 'bout I stand in for you over there so you can be here for Jerry."

"Sure, I can do that," he said.

"Okay, here's the big question: You and I both know that this isn't going to blow over or come to a good ending..."

"The woman knows the score," thought Davis.

"Can you take over for him in the pulpit?" she continued.

"What?"

"Sunday," she continued by way of explanation, "he preached from the parable of the Lost Sheep. Nothing wrong with that, but he pretty much broke down publicly. I care about him, but I also have to care about the congregation. We're going to have to be ready if something breaks, whether it's him or the situation. Would you be willing to act like the second pastor in Shelly's absence?"

The feelings all came flooding back– feelings of bearing responsibility for the living and the dead. He wanted to say, "No, I can't. I have a contract with the University that says I can't moonlight with a second job." The truth was, however, that the Department Chair was a man of compassion and understanding, and soon they would be between terms.

"Ella, if it were anyone but Jerry, the answer would be 'No,' but I am connected to this somehow. I have six weeks between Thanksgiving and New Year's. After that, I can't help!"

"Thank you, Davis. I know this isn't what you want... what am I saying, this is an absolute nightmare... but six weeks..." There was a pause. "Well, six weeks is beyond the end of the world."

Davis crossed the hall to Barstow's office. "Denton?" he said, knocking on the jam of the open door.

"Come on in," said Barstow.

"You asked earlier if I needed anything. The Presbytery wants me to work alongside Jerry until... well, until things resolve. I told them that I could help out during the weeks between fall and winter quarter."

"That shouldn't be a problem. Classes are not in session."

"Thanks, Denton. It's not something I want to do."

"Who would?"

The last item of business was to talk to Jerry. This time he was not calling as a friend, but as a potential usurper. That would not be Davis' intention, but in Ferguson's state of mind, the offer could destroy a new friendship. Later that afternoon, Davis called Jerry.

"Jerry?" began McGowan. "Has Ella Sanderson talked to you yet?"

"Yes, she seems to think that I need some help."

"Hey, I'm the one who needs help," bantered Davis. "I think she just knows that you need to have a little more flex in your time with everything else going on."

"That would be okay."

"But hey, you're calling the shots. I've seen that Peacemaker, so I'll do whatever you need."

"I don't tolerate slackers, McGowan."

"You're the boss! How 'bout I stop in tomorrow, and we can talk about it."

"Sounds good… and Davis… thanks!"

Chapter Nineteen

The Visitor

Davis was walking a fine line in his new position as a Parish Associate at St. Andrew's Church. It had been more than a month since Shelly Martin's mysterious disappearance, and almost all hope had waned along with the enthusiasm of those anxious to find an answer.

Jerry Ferguson had lost neither. For two Sundays in a row he had patterned his message on Jesus' parable of the lost sheep. Most people understood his paralysis of thought, but some complained that he should take a leave of absence until his head cleared. His response was a completely different text, but the same sentiment. He spoke of Jesus' admonition of "Seek and ye shall find."

Davis understood his friend, but also knew of the damage that his behavior could cause both to himself and to the congregation. A public pulpit is never the place to experience a private meltdown, and that was what they were all witnessing. Now that he had an official, albeit, temporary position at the church, he became a lightning rod for complaints. Congregation members would drop by his office to chat, and would invariably begin, "I know that Jerry is going through a rough time, but..." McGowan knew enough to discount everything before the "but". Even though it is not the first word of the sentence, "but" is always the first word of the message. The line was a fine one that ran between giving Jerry personal support and providing a path for those who were ready to try and find a way back to normal.

Families who suffer a loss like this always speak of the need for closure. McGowan had to begin assuming that such a thing might never actually come. To the extent that he could draw attention to himself, he would provide emotional privacy to his friend.

"Jerry, I just arrived on the scene and the people don't know me from Adam; do you think that I should preach next Sunday?" he asked.

"I was planning on continuing my series," said Ferguson, "but what you're saying makes sense. You probably won't be here very long, so it's best to maximize your participation and let you hit the ground running."

Davis breathed a sigh of relief. In fact, he thought he detected relief in Jerry's voice. This was a competent, caring man. He had to know, at some level, that there were growing rumbles in the peanut gallery.

"With Advent coming on maybe you should be the one to teach the Pastor's Bible Study, too? How often will we have a college professor on staff?"

McGowan started to go into his "I'm an instructor, not a professor" speech, but didn't want anything to challenge the basic concept. After a week in the new job, it was apparent that Jerry was surrendering most of the pastoral responsibilities to Davis.

"I need to be available in case something turns up," he rationalized. But there was more at stake. The newspapers had stopped asking questions, and the police relegated the case to a single investigator. If it wasn't technically a "cold case," it was, at least, tepid.

When Jerry's sister, Grace, announced that she was returning to Indianapolis to check on their father, Davis suggested that he go, too. "It's only two hours by car," he argued, "I think your father needs to see you to know you are okay."

In spite of his father's dementia, Jerry knew that there were days when he was lucid. "Maybe I should," he agreed. "But we'll take two cars in case I have to be back in a hurry."

The church board, the session, met hastily to approve a paid leave of absence. They genuinely hoped that in this respite Ferguson could find some path to peace. Realistically, they could not see a way to peace, but were relieved with Jerry's decision to take some time away.

The morning Grace and Jerry packed their cars to leave, Davis had a caller come to his office. He walked in off the street and specifically asked for McGowan. Since he had not given a name, the secretary could only say that there was a visitor waiting to see him. Davis walked out to the reception area to greet the guest whom he identified right away.

"Agent Abedinejad," he said. This time the man was dressed in a navy suit and a silver and blue striped tie.

"I thought I'd dress closer to your expectations; may we talk?"

Davis led him back into the private office.

"I've been here before. You haven't changed the décor much."

McGowan didn't know how to take the comment. He had met Agent Smith in the parking lot, but, of course, he had been in this room before. It was Shelly's office. Working out of her old office would not have been Davis' first choice, but it was the only space available once the police had declared it open.

"And I won't change it," he commented. "I'm only here temporarily, so I will leave it pretty much 'as is'."

"As fun as it would be to chat, I really came on

business. You seem to have an interest in the case and, quite frankly, we are only hitting dead ends."

"Dead ends? What about the call from Marlene Zeller or the email saying that Rad Finch had called the night Shelly vanished? What about the photo with all of them? Hell, by your own admission, you were in the picture!"

"Dr. McGowan, watch the language. We are in a church!" This last remark, in addition to being condescending, was confusing. In the parking lot of The Narrows, the agent had seemed open and sympathetic. Now, he had become his own evil twin.

"Let me start over, Davis; I didn't mean to make you defensive. The case, as it stands, is getting weaker as we look at the details. Do we have a photograph? No, we don't. For that matter, we have no email. Both Reverend Martin's and your computer were searched electronically, and nothing was found."

"How can that be?" protested Davis. "I showed you a printout, and I know that it came off my office computer."

"I am only telling you the results of our tests. Don't shoot the messenger, Dr. McGowan."

Davis could have strangled the man for either the tone or the content of his words. Both together, made the recovery of his own composure nearly impossible, but he, somehow, managed it.

"Even without all those things, there are public records that connect people. For example, Shelly Davis delivered the funeral homily for Marlene Zeller's mother."

"Yes, I understand that you called the chief of police with that tidbit. The problem, as it turns out, is that Marlene Zeller's mother is quite alive. In fact, she showed up in Dayton for her daughter's funeral. She was understandably upset. Being away from her home, she was referred to a local physician who gave her a prescription for a benzodiazepine. We have that information, so it didn't make much sense to pursue your wild-goose chase."

"My wild-goose chase?"

"You did tell us about the phone message on Ferguson's cell. You even said that you could hear it clearly."

"Yes, I could hear the message," said Davis.

"In that message did Reverend Martin say, 'Hello Jerry,' or 'Hi, Honey' or any other form of endearment?"

"No," said Davis.

"Didn't you think that odd, if this marriage was so idyllic?"

"I didn't think about it at all. She was in her work mode. Maybe there were people standing around when she called? There are some cell phone users who are conscious about what others can hear of their conversation."

"Jerry was conscious enough," said Smith, "he certainly let you hear his message."

"But..." Davis was cut off.

"The message was not hard to trace. It was right here at the church. It was called into the church office a couple of weeks prior to the night you heard it. Martin was telling the church secretary that she was going to the hospital to see an older woman name Bessie Hollows, who apparently had a stroke. There were no words of intimacy because it was not a message meant for him, and when he played it in the car, it was meant for you."

Davis' thoughts raced. He was scrambling to build an argument to counter what he was hearing. He could not deny the evidence, but he could not set it against what he knew about Shelly and Jerry.

"Someone else could have put that message on his phone. In fact, I heard the message ring in when we got back into an area that had a strong signal."

"It's good that you want to defend your friend, Dr. McGowan, but we know how it was done, and by whom. The whole thing was very low-tech. The message was recorded off the church's phone system on a small digital recorder. Ferguson had one in his pocket. He also had Shelly's cell phone, and that's the only conjecture that we have at this point. Just before you left camp, he called his cell phone on his wife's. Of course, his was turned off, so it went straight to voice mail."

"But he didn't receive a signal. Her phone is probably from the same provider; how could he have sent any message?"

"Did you actually turn on his phone and see if he was getting a signal?"

"No!" retreated Davis.

"Then, I suggest that you let me finish. He probably did this around the time you were going to leave so that the timing would be right." Davis couldn't remember any time when Jerry had slipped away, but he was not about to break the storyline. "He played the recorder through the phone, and his alibi was ready to be triggered during the ride home in the car. From my point of view, it would be easy to accomplish and fits the known facts."

"Facts? When Jerry and I left, Shelly was alive and well. She was standing in this office. That's a fact."

"That's the advantage of a murder that is premeditated. The witnesses get set up in advance of the action. If the opportunity for the crime passes, no one thinks anything about it. Suppose Jerry didn't murder Shelly that night when he got home? Would you have thought the phone call odd? You'd never ask about it again. It's only because she vanished that you think it's important now."

"Jerry Ferguson is not a murderer. Shelly was here when I drove past."

"You have no idea where she was, and you have no idea as to what happened after you dropped Ferguson at his house. All you know is that he couldn't get her on her cell phone. You thought it was because she had it turned off. Maybe he had it turned off and it was in his pocket."

"But..." The conjunction was the only thing left to Davis' argument. Unfortunately, he had nothing at the moment to say after it.

"Anything can be made to look like anything if you have the time, money, and intelligence to accomplish it," said Abedinejad. "That's the fact that matters!"

Chapter Twenty

===

Millett Hall

Davis didn't know whether it was the intensity of the parish responsibilities or the visit by Agent Smith, but he longed for some respite in the isolation of his windowless office. "The fact was," he rationalized, "that his temporary employment should not interfere with his educational calling."

He left his car in back of Millett Hall where he had the choice of hundreds of parking slots in a lot where open spaces were usually on the verge of extinction. He entered on the basement level and passed the computer lab. During class sessions, it was open around the clock, but now the glass door stood locked and the room only dimly lit for the sake of the surveillance cameras. The stairwell echoed with each of his steps as he climbed to the third floor.

It seemed odd to see the place so deserted, but, at the moment, it was a blissful alternative to the reminders at St. Andrew's. He used his pass key to enter the office area of the Department of Religion, and the door swung locked behind him. He checked his empty mailbox before realizing the futility of the gesture. "Who would have been here to take a message or sort the mail?" he thought.

His small office seemed warmly inviting as he unlocked the door and turned on the light. By the time his computer booted, his mind was already filtering through the changes he wanted to make in the winter quarter's syllabus. Within two hours he had saved and printed the document. In the printing room, he made a hundred-and-fifty collated and stapled copies with the push of a button. In the end, he looked with satisfaction on the stack of papers that would be waiting for him on the first day of class.

He took the papers back to the office, but found, when it came down to it, that the place was hard to leave. He pulled a few books off the shelves. Some were free samples that he had collected from publishers; others were titles that related to the pastoral activities which characterized his past life, not his present one. In a moment of clarity, he added them to the pile. Books are difficult to throw away. They are easier to give to a good home, so he decided to place these up for adoption. Pulling on his outer jacket, he lifted the stack and headed out of the office area. His destination was a table in the tunnels between University and Allyn Halls. It was a place where books could be left to fend for themselves and were free to any taker. McGowan had left books there before and found them gone a day later. With winter break, they would crowd the space a little while, but would, soon enough, find their way out.

Halfway to the stairwell, he wished that he had planned two trips, but it really wasn't all that far. At some point, Seward Hiltner's book on pastoral care slid from the top of the pile and flew to a lower landing. The crash reverberated through the shaft, but the book waited patiently at the bottom for Davis to restore it to the collection.

It was when he bent over to pick it up that he became aware of a footfall on the steps above. At first he doubted his senses, but then tested his doubt. Having regained the volume he started down the final flight to the basement level. Halfway, he stopped mid-stride. The other foot on the stair finished the step with a sound that could not be denied.

"A paranoid person would call out," thought McGowan. "For that matter, a sane one might as well." Davis just hurried down the rest of the way and made the quick turn into the tunnel. If anyone was following, surely they would expect him to go out the way he came in, through the parking lot.

Once in the tunnel, he made the cut over toward the main corridor that led to University Hall. He knew the system and was quickly unloading the books on the table. Once, he looked back and thought he caught a glimpse of another person coming around the corner where he had just been, but when he looked again, no one was there. Of course, that made it worse. An innocent in the tunnel would not step back out of sight.

McGowan thought better of taking the same route back. He took the corridor that led to Allyn Hall. There he passed by the campus security office and was relieved that it was open and an armed campus cop was monitoring the desk. Davis waved as he passed.

He flew up the stairs, crossed over to Millett on the first floor, and then took an out-of-the-way stairwell at the northwest corner of the building to the parking area. Once outside, he faced the same nearly empty lot that he had entered a few hours before. A twist of the key, and his car came to life. A mile later, his pulse returned to normal.

Chapter Twenty-One

Bessie Hollows

The challenge for McGowan was to redirect his thinking. He had almost forgotten that the key to pastoral ministry was the ability to switch activities quickly and seamlessly. He remembered one particular Saturday when he left a graveside service at noon to officiate at a wedding at one-thirty. Maintaining focus was the key. One of the most valuable tools, in his opinion, was an automobile. Until the invention of cell phones, cars were the perfect isolation booth. To be all alone with one's own thoughts or with music was a way to adjust the grip on reality. Because of this, Davis was relieved when Brenda, the church secretary, appeared at his office door to say that the hospital had called to report that Bessie Hollows had been admitted.

He had heard that name before. He had heard Shelly's voice speaking it through a voice message on Jerry's cell phone. If Agent Smith was correct, that message was some sort of ploy, but this was real. Up to this moment, Bessie Hollows was just a name, an extra piece of a puzzle; now she would become a real person to Davis. Still, he could not help but think that if what the agent said were true, then all of his intuition and experience with Ferguson was a fraud. That was an unacceptable conclusion. That, however, had to be pushed aside to allow an old woman to be the focus of attention. "Thank goodness for the sanctuary of the automobile." He turned off his cell phone as he went out to the car.

The drive to the hospital was firing old neural pathways in McGowan's head. Ministers spend many hours in hospital halls and develop patterns of where to park and how to best get in and out of the facility. After several years of teaching at the university, he imagined that building projects and additions to the hospital might require changes in his parking routine. As it turned out, however, the former path proved true and he took a parking ticket at the Apple Street parking garage. He drove up through the helix of parked cars to the level where he could walk directly to the elevated walkway that led him straight to the visitor's desk.

He had never met Bessie Hollows' family, but he knew, at least, that her son's name was Randy. That was a start. Hospital visits were always an exercise in improvisation. He remembered being told once that, for patients, the minister represents something from a world more familiar to a patient than the alien space of a hospital bed. An overnight stay in a care facility nearly always raises questions of mortality. Davis expected that more promises are made to God in the corridors and rooms of medical facilities than in most churches, synagogues, or mosques. Like the illness, however, most patients are able to put such things behind them after discharge. Still, the pastoral visit could take a variety of forms from his being the clown to a mediator between heaven and earth. The cue to appropriate behavior is given in the initial encounter with the patient or the family. Some rooms are festive with balloons while others are as quiet as death itself. Bessie's room was like death.

Upon entering, Davis saw a diminutive form, open-eyed and staring at the ceiling. In a corner of the dim room sat a thirty-something couple. The man stood as McGowan entered.

"I am Davis McGowan from the church," he said, extending his right hand.

"I recognized you from Sunday; I am Randy and this is my wife, Trisha." The woman nodded. Davis could see that she had been crying moments earlier. The brief exchange told him that these were members with more commitment than the Christmas and Easter crowd.

"How is your mother doing?" he asked.

"The doctor said that she had another stroke. She

gets her words mixed up when she talks and she can't move her right arm much."

Davis walked over to the bed and spoke to Bessie. She turned her eyes to meet his. "Hi, I'm Davis. I just started at the church this last week. I'm helping my friend, Reverend Ferguson, while he's going through this rough period." Tears rolled from the corner of her eyes, and Davis instinctively took a tissue from the box on the tray table and touched it to her cheek to absorb the moisture.

"I know Shelly was a friend of yours, too," he offered, realizing that he had spoken in the past tense.

The woman began to speak, her words distinct though slurred. "She was so very ketchup." Her face contorted with the odd words. "Clean," she said, and then she pursed her quivering lips.

"It's okay," said Davis. "I think I know what you mean, she is very kind. She is very loving."

Bessie's features softened. Her head nodded agreement and she sank back into the pillow with a look of relief.

"Do you know what happened to you?" asked McGowan. Without waiting for an answer, he went into an explanation. "You had another stroke and this has affected your speech. You know exactly what you want to say, but the wrong word comes out, right?" Bessie nodded. "You can't fool me, though," he added, "I know you're in there." With those words he stroked her cheek softly. She turned her head and kissed his hand. It surprised McGowan.

"Did you know Randy and Trisha are here?" he asked her. She shook her head. "They're right here!" He gestured for them to join him at the bedside. "See!" He indicated and she turned her head to see them, her eyes brightened, and Davis could see that there was affection between the three.

"Hi, Mom," said Randy, and Trisha placed a palm on her mother-in-law's cheek.

"I'll bet you didn't know they were hiding over there!"

"I didn't sew the cushion," she struggled to get the words out, and frustration came flooding back.

"It's okay," McGowan said softly. "We know that the ideas are straight in your mind; the words just don't come out right. It will take time, but that can improve. Right now it's our job to guess a little about what you mean. You can nod to us when we it get right?"

She nodded.

"But you have the hardest job, and that is to not get so frustrated that you think that we don't love you!" A half-smile was all her ravaged body could afford, but it was all she needed.

"We do love you, Mom!" It was Trisha speaking.

The four joined hands and Davis said a short

prayer. Afterward, he looked at Randy and said, "I imagine that they are keeping her blood thin and watching to see if she regains her speech and muscle control."

"Yes," said Randy. "They say that we will know better in a few days, but the doctor has already ordered therapy."

"Did you hear that, Bessie?" The woman's eyes shifted back from her son to Davis. "The doctors are going to adjust your blood thinners. You'll probably have bruises, but that's just the medicine. And they will get you into therapy. They are going to help you learn to get your words straight again. They do amazing things, but you're going to have to stick with us."

Bessie nodded.

"I am going to go now, but I'll be back. I'd rather see you seated with your family in church," he offered.

"Bargain," said Bessie. Davis didn't know if he was hearing another wrong word or Bessie was suggesting a deal. He didn't care. It was an opportunity.

"It would be the best bargain we could hope for! You back with your family! I'll see you soon!"

Davis stepped back from the bed and made eye contact with Randy who followed him out to the corridor.

"Your mother is very alert," he said.

"I can see that now," said Randy.

"Patients don't see themselves lying in bed; they only see us. Because we look the same, for them nothing has changed that much. But if they see us being afraid, well, they pick up on our discomfort. They see it in our faces. It took me awhile to figure that out. Once I realized that, I decided that the real trick was to look past the tubes and wires and see the person I knew rather than the sickness that has them down. Your Mom is still there, so you and Trisha's job is to look for her and let the docs look at the stroke. Watch the nurses. The really good ones will walk in the room and tell her about the weather and what's going to happen next. It's their way of reminding her that they know she's alive. Because she can't join in on the conversation, sometimes people will start talking around her. You're her life-line. Keep her informed, and for now, keep questions 'yes' and 'no'. She can answer those. Now, I might get arrested for practicing medicine without a license, if I say much more, so this conversation never actually happened."

"Thanks, Dr. McGowan."

"Davis."

"Thanks, Davis. Is there any word on Reverend Shelly?"

"I'm afraid not. Jerry has gone over to Indianapolis for a few days with his sister. They are going to be checking on his father who is in a nursing home there."

"Funny," began Randy, "we're sitting here thinking about my mother and the people who come to visit her might be doing the same for their parents. Shelly was the kindest person I ever saw. My Mom really took to her."

"We all did, Randy. Shelly is exceptional... so is Jerry. They both are, and you're right, they have both been through a lot. They won't tell you about it, but it has made them who they are."

"Well, thanks again, Davis. I'd better get back to Mom. Tell her about the weather or the cat."

"You got it!" said Davis, "and I will be back."

He turned down the hall and walked past the elevators to the stairwell and walked down the five flights to the ground floor. It was an odd feeling to be in the hospital again. It was like visiting someone else's life that had become his own, again.

Chapter Twenty-two

Paranoia

McGowan's friends sometimes accused him of being overly analytical, and perhaps he was. His defense followed the same genetic logic as any healthy adolescent. It was his parents' fault.

Davis came from a different background than many of his clergy colleagues. It took him by surprise in seminary that many fellow students had fathers who were also ordained. With the acceptance of women in church leadership roles, it became even more obvious that the ministerial vocation was known to run in families. This was not true in McGowan's case. His father did not have a college education, but became a telephone engineer in a time when companies would train and promote people based on performance rather than a paper trail of diplomas. His sister was a mathematician, his youngest brother was an electrical engineer, and the brother closest to his own age was a cartoonist. The combination of this genetic code meant that he did not have a chance. McGowan tended toward organizing ideas into logical patterns of problem-solving that sometimes jumped out of the box. Some of the problems were invitations to his creative side and satisfying. Shelly's disappearance was not one of those, but it was one that he could not leave to others to solve.

As he crossed over the walkway back to his parked car, he asked himself why he was in such a hurry to get back to the office. His job here was finished, but staying in the building was a perfect excuse for keeping the cell phone off and the rest of the world at bay. He decided to go to the car, get the yellow legal pad that was sitting in the back seat, and return to the hospital and sit in some obscure corner where no one would call on him.

Some people have an aversion to hospitals, but being comfortable in one is part of a minister's turf. At the same time, they are very private public places. Even crowded waiting rooms are havens of solitude. Patients waiting to be called for tests and family members waiting to hear from surgeons become islands of quiet concern. Davis was going to find a spot and make his own island.

When he reached the parking garage, he went through the glass doors and walked up the slope to where he had left his car. The outside air was cool but then again, it was December. He hit the button on his keychain twice and heard the soft click as the door latches released. The engine of a car parked a little further up on the ramp fired as Davis reached into the back seat to get what he called his "think pad." He withdrew the paper, slammed the door, and hit the lock button. The solid thunk of the mechanism told him that the doors had locked.

As he walked toward the rear of his car he paused as the up-ramp auto backed out of the space. The license plate caught McGowan's eye. It was a vanity plate featuring the bald eagle and the identifiers D-8-S-T-A-M-P. "Date Stamp?" thought Davis. He and Beth always played the game of trying to guess the meaning of the special plates. In this case, his mind went back to his early years in Dayton. "Monarch" was a big employer in Dayton. Many of the company executives had belonged to Covenant Church where he had been pastor for many years. They had pioneered postage meters, but had, long ago, been acquired in a corporate merger. Davis wondered whether D8STAMP was someone he would have recognized from those years.

He went back across the causeway to the hospital and took a right turn before the Outpatient Admissions. He followed the corridor back to Radiology where he knew there was a large waiting room. Going inside, he found the room less than half full and settled down into one corner of the room near the television that hung from a bracket on the wall. After taking off his coat and unfolding the copy of the email he had from Shelly Martin, he found himself facing a blank sheet of ruled paper.

The problem with solving any problem is figuring out the categories and defining a unit of measure. The engineer part of his brain was taking over. He decided that he was going to be making something that looked like a flow chart, that is, a series of boxes. From the boxes there would be arrows flowing to other boxes. The arrows would be labeled "If this, then this" and "If not this, then this." Now he was in the range of philosophy. "It is a simple matter of logic," he thought. The problem, of course, was naming the first box to determine what the units would be in this less-than-mathematical theory. Then it struck him, and struck him as humorous, that the boxes on his chart should be in units called "boxes."

Shelly had said as much in their first long conversation. Everything that Shelly told him needed to fit. When he thought of something that would not fit, he'd write it in a margin for later. He drew a box in the upper left hand corner of the paper. In it he wrote the first question, "What is a box?"

"A house is a box; it's even an empty box that can be sold!" That was part of Shelly's earlier conversation. This part of the puzzle was too easy to be interesting. It was well-documented in the burst of the housing bubble. Houses were sold. More houses were sold than ought to have been because more buyers were approved for loans that they could not afford. Every new loan created a set of fees at each step along the way. "Okay," thought Davis, "this is not about people selling homes; this is about making mortgages, and every mortgage generates closing costs for the lender. The seller takes away any equity from years of ownership, and the bank builds a new mortgage. If the new mortgage requires almost nothing down, origination fees and points can be set even higher. The new mortgage will be larger than the previous one because the new owner doesn't have any real equity in the property. The house isn't worth any more, but the mortgage is. Now the house isn't the empty box, people live there. The mortgage is the new box."

He remembered getting a letter from the mortgage company saying that their loan on the house in Fairborn had been sold to another lender. In other words, someone had literally sold and bought their mortgage while they were unaware. The house didn't change hands, but the mortgage did.

He looked at the last email from Shelly. *Value moves in transactions, not boxes* and *Value does not disappear, it moves*, were two of her points. Just then Davis was distracted by a flicker in the room light. He realized it came from quick images flashing on the TV over his head. He recognized it as one of those annoying commercials inviting people to turn in their old junk gold and silver jewelry for cash.

"That's another box," he thought. "How stupid would anyone be to fall for that! What they are saying is so dumb. 'Turn your gold and silver into precious paper!' Then again, enough people must do it to make it worth buying ads!" He underlined Shelly's words, "Value does not disappear, it moves."

This last thought became an epiphany for Davis. The problem will be solved by looking for value shifts. Every time the box shifts, value moves off in a different direction. Eventually, the box is empty. An empty box is one that no longer has a resident owner, and is not worth what is owed on the mortgage. The one who wrote the mortgage may be okay if it has been sold to someone else already. "What was it that Shelly said about that Christmas party?" thought McGowan.

You can sell empty boxes for higher prices, just don't look inside... the one who opens the box is the loser, it was something like that. But this, too, was a part of business news. Mortgages, good and bad, had been bundled like low-risk securities and validated by the ratings companies so that no one would or could look inside. And, eventually the boxes were stacked on shelves in neat rows in the investment portfolios of the average person's retirement savings. Of course, the people who stacked the boxes neatly were a part of the same system that cashed in on the last transaction. Once there, they could be safely opened to show that the value was almost all gone; it had flowed away in transaction after transaction.

Outrage is a much overrated emotion. It creates the illusion of action, but it is an energy release that potentially prevents a much larger event. It is not unlike the passive flood control system that protects Dayton, Ohio is actually a system that encourages the flooding of places off the beaten path. The public outrage of the economic downturn of 2008 and 2009 amounted to name calling and angry outbursts by people who had no real power except to look again into the empty boxes and see if any value had returned.

For example, an outraged public called Rad Finch "short-sighted, narcissistic, incompetent, and wasteful." His parachute deployed nicely, however, and, like an extraordinary magician, his final trick was to pull nine million little rabbits out of a nearly empty hat. An executive in a defunct bank, in a flood control effort, explained that he would give a "substantial amount" of his eight million dollar severance to a charitable foundation. Davis wondered what that would mean. To the average person $80,000 would be substantial. To the bailing exec it was only one percent. "Would that come with a paid seat on the foundation's board?" wondered McGowan. "He could get all his money back for attending charitable meetings."

For all of Davis' scribbling, there was nothing new here except the standard ruse, "It's good work if you can find it. If only we could all get rich by being fired for incompetence."

The problem, as McGowan saw it, was that it just didn't add up mathematically. These were not incompetent people. Shelly said the same and she knew them all on a different level than Davis. They had to prove themselves all the way up to the top levels of management. They had to argue their worth in high salaries and make parachutes a part of the standard package. Public outrage over their incompetence was the real lie. These people could not be what they seemed. Davis suspected that he had crossed over a cultural line. It didn't make sense because he was not seeing it from their perspective.

Of course, that's what Washington and so many were saying about the excesses of corporate America. "They were out of touch with the real America!"

"Were they?" asked Davis. He was reminded of the Native Americans who had been offered wampum beads for the purchase of Manhattan Island. To Europeans, at the time, these native peoples seemed too simple to know the value of property. To the Native Americans, who had no concept of land owner-ship in their culture, these strangers were offering money for nothing. The surprise came when the Europeans put up fences and started shooting.

In the modern case, there was nothing besides the simple war of words. The boxes were empty; the value was gone. But if the Elkhorn folk were right, the value had simply been moved or frittered away in corporate jets and lavish redecorating of office suites. "Out of touch, yes," thought Davis, "but not illegal." Then he realized why it was important that the boxes *not stink*. "Of course," said Davis forget-ting where he was. Some of the people waiting in radiology looked at him, but he went on in silence. "You try to empty the box as best you can, and for-get about shareholders, shift the value, but never il-legally. A Ponzi scheme empties boxes, but fills prison cells. The rules say empty the boxes, but only by legal means. They don't get stinky, and you don't get arrested."

Davis was thinking well outside his own set of boxes by now. He wrote "Ganesha" in the upper margin of the page. The Elkhorn people are a sub-culture that understands reality differently. "They wanted to lose money for investors, but how could that make sense?"

Davis put his pen to the paper and wrote, "401(k) plans are a box."

He gave that idea some thought. When the retirement savings box gets full enough, people start drawing on Social Security and leave the work force. Making the decision to retire is something else. To lose the security of a paycheck is one of the most difficult things in life to do. Davis had heard that at the meeting at Kirkmont. His friends were now planning to work longer because of economic fears.

And, there it was, an answer! The age of retirement had just been increased from 65 to... to whenever you could no longer go to work. Shelly's response to the plaque in his office came back to him: "There are two kinds of people in the world, those who can afford to retire and those who only think they can."

What are the great fears of the free enterprise system? "Socialism and the redistribution of wealth are two," thought Davis. "How about a government that commits to coming to the aid of the majority?" That was a scary thought, but so were all these ideas. The scariest was that they might not be something as simple as paranoia.

Davis wrote one last thing on the page: "'Elkhorn Institute' is a box." He knew that was true, and he knew it was entirely empty. Nothing stinky would be found there. Nothing illegal ever took place there. Money that passed through the town was clean. Its product was ideas, ideas that framed, what was to most, an alien culture. He was sure that they would call it the American Dream. McGowan saw it as a nightmare.

He drew a circle around the name "Ganesha."

Chapter Twenty-three

The Long Way Home

It was a little past three o'clock when Davis stood up from his chair in the radiology waiting room. His mind was clear. For all the twists and turns of his logic, he, at least, felt that he was coming to some clearer understanding of what might be happening around him. Even though she lived in Elkhorn, Shelly knew virtually nothing of the Institute or its mission. What she did know was the web of relationships that stretched invisibly between the alumni of Elkhorn who had become leaders of corporations. That knowledge had triggered unforeseen consequences. He knew now that these were cautious people and there would be no identifiable scheme or the smoking gun of a conspiracy. There was, however, a culture of like-mindedness engendering the same behavior patterns independently across the country.

"For those of you who have been enjoying this mild December weather, hold on to your hats!" The weather reporter on the TV was standing before a map. He gestured wildly as if indicating the severity of the approaching storm. "Over the next twelve to eighteen hours, we are going to see a front come through with our coldest temperatures of the season. And, yes, we are expecting snow! Our long range forecasts show a white Christmas on the horizon, but Santa may be coming a little sooner with a day off school for the kids. More at the five o'clock news hour!"

Davis pulled on his coat and went down the hall toward the exit and the way out to the parking garage. At the toll booth, he showed his clergy pass for the first time in years. He wondered if the nearly twenty-year-old photo still resembled him enough to pass scrutiny. Evidently it did, because the gate opened and he made a left turn on Apple Street. He took Brown Street to Wyoming. As he was passing the cemetery, a car that had been parking parallel to the street pulled out into traffic just ahead of him. It stopped at the light on Wayne Avenue immediately in front of Davis. It had a blue-gray metallic finish, and a license plate that read "D8STAMP."

"What are the odds?" said Davis. "Paranoid people do have enemies," he reminded himself.

The light turned green and the car ahead went straight through the intersection. Without signaling, McGowan took a right turn on Wayne Avenue and went up the hill to where Wilmington Pike split to the right. On the left was the inpatient unit of Dayton Hospice. He had visited patients there many times, but now he just wanted to use a parking space. He parked the car and walked into the building. He took a seat in the front corridor near a window where he could watch cars entering the lot. In less than five minutes, a blue-gray car pulled in. It drove directly to the row where McGowan's car was parked and drove slowly past, choosing a space one row over.

Davis felt in his jacket pocket for his cell phone.

Whoever D8STAMP was, he had to be following an electronic signal, otherwise, he would not have found the car so quickly. The unit also had to be in the car and not a trace on the cell phone which was still in his pocket.

Students always wanted to know how long you had to wait for an instructor who was late for class. Davis needed to think about how long his new friend would expect to wait on a minister paying a visit on a dying parishioner. At ten minutes, he decided to put D8STAMP out of his misery. This time he did not try to lose his companion. He went back to Wayne Avenue and turned right. As he approached the light at Smithville, the blue car slowed down. Davis thought of pulling over to wait but figured that D8STAMP might not have a sense of humor.

As he approached the church parking lot, McGowan's tagalong turned off. Evidently, his mission was to safely escort Davis home. "Mission accomplished!" said Davis as he walked into the church. He checked for phone messages, and filled Brenda in on the condition of Bessie Hollows.

"She's showing some paralysis, and her speech is affected, but Randy and Trisha are there and she seems calm. I think I'll stop down to see her tomorrow, too, that is, unless the snow socks us in." He went back to his office and sat at his desk. He took a long look around the room.

The encounter with D8STAMP made him think about the possibility of invisible realities. On that first morning when Jerry had awakened him with a phone call, Officer Collins said that this room was bugged. Of course that made perfect sense given the fact that the only thing missing was a photograph of Shelly and her friends at a luau. Whoever took it did not have to search or ransack anything. Shelly had said that she would make a list, two lists, in fact. Were they with the photo? Why would Shelly make two lists and keep them in the same place? If the place were bugged on that first morning, couldn't it still be monitored? Who would be listening? Finch? Smith? Maybe there's no real difference between them. Smith certainly acted differently on the second visit than he had when they were sitting in

McGowan's car at The Narrows.

Davis pulled open the center drawer of the desk and stared at the empty corner where he had seen Shelly place the photo. The only thing in its place was a small tourist souvenir of the Holy Land, a small paper scroll of the prophet Isaiah.

"How stupid!" said McGowan, and then he stopped himself from talking aloud in a room that might have both ears and eyes. The most ancient and complete scroll of the prophet Isaiah was a well-known part of the Dead Sea Scrolls. If the souvenir scroll was in the desk, what was hidden away in the pottery jar on Shelly's bookshelf? The Dead Sea Scrolls were successfully hidden for nearly two thousand years; that's where Martin would have kept her second copy of a secret list.

The immediate problem was to retrieve the pottery jar without raising suspicion. He put the scroll back in the center drawer, stood and went to the bookshelves where the shofar, the Roman coins, and the pottery model of the scroll jar were displayed. He picked up a coin and studied it. Carefully, he put it back. He did the same with the ram's horn. Finally, he stepped toward the office door and called to the secretary.

"Brenda, do you think it would be all right if I used some of Shelly's props for the junior sermon on Sunday?"

"What?" said the woman with surprise. She was not accustomed to being asked about the content of the service.

"Shelly has these things that might be appealing to the kids, but I don't know them well enough to be sure."

Brenda came to the door, "What's that, Davis?"

"I'm thinking that this is Advent, a season of expectation; and well... take this for example..." McGowan picked up the pottery jar. "The ancient priests hid treasures in them, well they were a lot bigger, near the Dead Sea. They stayed hidden for centuries. So you have these plain looking vessels with treasures inside." As he went on, Davis thought he was going to gag on the insipidness of his own suggestion.

"Uh, that sounds good," said Brenda.

McGowan looked into her confused face and just wanted to say, "Bless you for agreeing with that blarney!" Instead he said, "Do you think it's okay if I use this even though it belongs to Shelly?"

A thoroughly confused Brenda offered, "I suppose it's okay. Sure, she wouldn't mind!"

"Thanks, Brenda, you've been a big help. I'm kinda coming into all this blind and it's good to have someone like you around who knows the people." Brenda returned to her own work area and Davis hoped that her remembrance of his strange idiocy wouldn't stay with her too long. He went back to his own desk and opened a book to read. He did not want to look to be hurrying out of the office, but when he left, he would carry a pottery jar with him.

Chapter Twenty-four

Language Barrier

As Davis started the engine, he wondered if D8STAMP would suddenly appear. Of course if someone had attached a GPS tracking device somewhere on his car, they would not need to follow along as long as he was riding along predictable paths. The route between St. Andrew's and his home in Fairborn was probably on D8STAMP's safe list. He knew that his movements were being tracked by someone, and yet, he didn't know to what extent that might be true. It occurred to him that there was another test which could drive out the argument that he was just plain paranoid.

Instead of driving north to the Interstate, he took a left turn on Trebein and drove out into the country. At Beaver Valley Road, he turned left and came into Fairborn near the old K-Mart Plaza. He parked the car and went into the store.

"Thank you," he said aloud when the familiar blue-gray car showed up a few minutes later. As odd as it seemed, knowing that he was being followed gave McGowan a certain peace of mind. The facts in this case, he felt, gave him permission to be completely paranoid. If the office was bugged and his movements were being watched, where else could he expect surveillance? His house would certainly be a target. He felt that he was now living in the book *1984*.

He and Beth were not always scrupulous about locking doors. That would be clear to anyone watching their comings and goings. Besides that, McGowan felt that a standard lockset would not impede the people whom he was dealing with. His house was bugged. It was not paranoia; it was a practical assumption based on an inference from the specific to the general. It was inductive logic. "Thank you, Mr. Aristotle," said the voice of the philosopher in his head.

He looked around the store and bought a cheap headset for his computer. D8STAMP would see him emerge from the store with a bag in hand. "If I am going to be a paranoid," he said to himself, "I am going to be a cautious one."

From the store it was a short trip up Maple Avenue to home. Davis took the pottery jar that he had lain on the front seat and added it to the contents of the plastic bag with the headset. He walked into the house and set the package down on the kitchen table. He was playing to a microphone, maybe even a camera, for all he knew. He wanted his performance to be credible, unhurried, and unremarkable. "In other words," he thought, "act like myself."

Beth was coming up the basement steps when he called to her. "How about a glass of wine before dinner?" he asked.

"Bad day?" she queried.

"Not particularly. I got to meet Bessie Hollows. She had another stroke, but seems stable. She's a sweetie and has a nice family.

"I just don't have a meeting tonight and thought we could just relax a little. There's a little more than two weeks until Christmas, and the biggest thing for me is to figure out how to use a pottery jar for a junior sermon."

Beth laughed, "that should be easy enough. Isn't the answer to the minister's question always 'Jesus'?"

They both laughed. It was an old joke about the minister who asked the children: "What has a bushy tail, lives in a tree, and gathers nuts for the winter?"

A child thinks for a moment and says, "It sounds like a squirrel, but I know it has to be Jesus!"

"No Jesus here," said Davis. "And, I'm thinking scrolls, not squirrels." He went to the table and withdrew the pottery urn from the bag. He didn't open it for fear that the dining area would be the logical focus for a remote observer. Instead, he went and sat on the end of the sofa farthest away from the reading lamp. He lifted the lid. There was a rolled piece of paper inside. All reason told him that this jar was designed to house the Isaiah scroll in Shelly's desk drawer. If he was right, it would be her notes in some protective guise to throw off the curious. He was right.

Carefully, he opened the scroll and could not help but laugh out loud.

"What is it?" asked Beth.

"It's a joke scroll, that's all."

"What do you mean?"

"Listen," began Davis who started to read from the curling paper in his hand. "The oldest manuscripts of the New Testament are written in uncial script. The word 'uncial' means 'a twelfth part'. This name is derived from the fact that they are written in lines of about twelve characters."

"Wow, that's hilarious," said Beth sarcastically. "Exactly how much have you had to drink?"

"No, that's not the funny part. The funny part is the sample writing. Usually they'd put something like the opening words to John's Gospel which are: ΕΝ ΑΡΧΗ ΗΝ 'Ο ΛΟΓΟΣ, but look what's written here instead."

Beth came over and settled in beside him.

"That's still Greek, Dear!"

"Oh," bantered Davis, "I keep forgetting that you

are a non-Greek speaker. In the old days, we called them barbarians!"

"What's the joke, Plato?" she said.

"Look," he said taking one of his calling cards and pulling a pen from his pocket. He turned the card over to the blank side and wrote, "Laugh a little after you read this."

Beth chuckled on cue.

"It says ΕΙΣ ΑΦΕΔΡΩΝΑ which means 'into the toilet.' Jesus did say that, but it usually gets cleaned up in translation."

Now Beth laughed, but it would be some time before Davis would tell her that the message was not written in Greek at all. Shelly had left a clear note. The words were English, but written in Greek characters and the first three words jumped out at Davis: ΘΕΕΛΚΟΡΝΙΝΣΤΙΤΥΤΕ. In English letters, it read "The Elkhorn Institute." What followed was a list of names which would have to be deciphered later.

** ** **

That evening after dinner Davis phoned Jerry Ferguson who was staying with his sister in Indianapolis.

"Just thought that you should be brought up-to-date on what's happening," began McGowan. "Bessie Hollows was readmitted to the hospital, but

I think she's going to be okay. They're going to give her therapy." He omitted the fact that there had been a second stroke, but he wanted Jerry not to feel rushed if he needed more time away.

"Davis, I've been one major slacker the last few weeks. I think it's time I got back up on the horse."

'Whatever you say, Jerry, it's your call."

"I'm going to drive across tomorrow so that I can be in the service on Sunday."

"Fair enough," answered Davis. "Have you heard the weather report?"

"Yes, but it's Interstate all the way and they should have that plowed. I won't leave until after the morning rush hour, so it'll be under control."

"Well, take it easy. If it's really bad, you could wait until Saturday and still be in church. Why don't you come over here to the house for dinner tomorrow, or Saturday, if that's when you get back in town? We can touch base about Sunday morning."

"Sounds like a plan," he answered. "And when Shelly gets home, I promise that we'll have you and Beth over for chili or something."

"Will I need to bring my antacid for your chili?"

"Of course, it wouldn't be chili if it weren't hot!"

Davis groaned at the bad pun. "It will be good to have you back, Jerry. Drive carefully, and see you tomorrow."

"How does he sound?" asked Beth as he clicked

off the phone.

"He sounds fine, but I don't think he's doing so well. He's invited us for dinner as soon as Shelly gets back."

"Oh," said Beth.

Chapter Twenty-five

Avalanche

As promised, the morning news was punctuated by school closings running along the bottom of the screen. During the night the city was stopped by an avalanche of snow. In Dayton, like many other cities, the task of clearing the roads was often left until after the snow had stopped. As a strategy, this is efficient and effective for light showers, but creates chaos with heavier events. Having grown up in the Cleveland area, McGowan knew that the best strategy was to assume that every snowfall would be heavy and begin continuous plowing as soon as possible after the first flake.

In spite of the flurry over the weather, another story caught Davis by surprise. "Police report that a body was discovered yesterday in a wooded area near The Narrows in Beavercreek. Authorities have not released any information, but there is speculation that it might be the body of Reverend Shelly Martin who was reported missing more than a month ago."

Switching between channels, Davis stayed glued to the TV, but news was sparse and speculation was rampant. Evidently hikers had come across body parts indicating that animals had been at the corpse. Police forensics had cordoned off the area, but the snow was hampering investigation.

"Who else could it be?" asked Davis for the third time.

"Poor Jerry," said Beth. "I wonder if he's picked up on the news."

"If he has, you know he'll drive over regardless of the road conditions."

Breakfast was silent that morning, and Davis decided that he would take to the road. "People will be calling the church," he said. "I want to be there when they do."

The fifteen minute drive took a little over forty-five minutes and the parking lot wasn't plowed. Most snow removal contracts put churches high on the Sunday list and low on the weekdays. This was Friday, and McGowan doubted that a plow would come through until Saturday. Even before leaving the house, he had already called the staff telling them not to come into the office. Like Davis, they were concerned about the news.

"I'll be there," he said. "If conditions don't improve, I'll set the main number to call forward to my house. Enjoy your day off with your kids," he said to Brenda.

"Thanks," she said. "All day with teenagers, why do you think I want to come in to work?"

"At least the sense of humor survives the news," thought Davis.

His car plowed through the snow as he pulled into the church lot. He stopped at the parking space closest to the road in case he had to shovel his way out later. The rest of the way to the building was done on foot with knee-high drifts creeping up the inside of his pant legs on each step. He stomped his feet hard when he reached the protected area under the canopy. He fumbled for the keys and unlocked the door. He was the only one in the building, but he chose to leave the door unlocked against the possibility that someone might come by.

His optimism was not unfounded. Sam Parker showed up in his pickup truck with a plow mounted on the front.

"Hey, Rev," he said, after cutting a swath to the door. "I saw your car and figured you might need a little help. Is your car stuck there?"

"I don't think so, Sam. I just pulled in that far in case I have to fight to get out."

"Well, you should be able to get out now. Can't do much more than a little path though. My truck'll handle driveways, but a parking lot with this much snow would blow out my engine."

"They'll get it cleared by Sunday. Say, can I pay you something for your trouble?"

"Nah, that's fine. I just saw your car and figured that I sure wouldn't want to get snowed in at a church. Maybe a bar, no offense meant."

"None taken, Sam. I think I'd rather be stuck in a bar, too. Of, course, I'd only be there to convert the sinners," he added.

"Sort of a 'last call for drinks,' then!"

"Good one, Sam. Thanks for your help."

The phone didn't ring much. Either the snow or the lack of specificity in the news reporting had discouraged it, or a combination of the two. Davis was about to enter the code to forward phone calls to his home when a visitor appeared at the door.

"Agent Smith," he said, rising from behind the desk. The man walked into the office and took a seat in one of the chairs that faced McGowan's desk.

"What brings you to the office in this weather, Dr. McGowan?" he began.

"Probably the same thing that brings you," he answered, "the morning news."

"In that regard," said Smith, "I know more than you've heard, but not, maybe, more than you have guessed."

"What do you know?" Davis asked.

"What do you guess?" came the retort. The two looked at each other, neither wishing to be the first to break. "I'll tell you what," said Smith, "we'll alternate. I will go first. The body found two days ago was that of Shelly Martin."

"Two days ago?"

"Yes, two days. We know who it is from clothing and other identification. We've had dental records for quite some time. Of course, the news reports will be full of disclaimers about the need for DNA tests, but, in this case, that's just the nonsense people expect to hear."

"So, she was already lying dead in The Narrows the day we were sitting in the parking lot talking."

"Probably," said the agent. "Of course the case could be made that Ferguson might have moved the body there later."

"Jerry? You've got to be kidding. You know he didn't kill Shelly, much less move her body after she turned up missing. He was a basket case."

"Remember that I told you that anything could be made to look like anything. Maybe your friend is a better actor than you." Davis wondered what that last comment meant in light of his own performance at the Greek theater the night before. "What is your take on events, Dr. McGowan?"

Davis took a deep breath. "Who are you?" he asked.

"That's not really fair, is it? It was my turn to ask the question. On the other hand, I can give you a cryptic answer if that's what you need to loosen your tongue."

Davis felt played.

"When I was introduced to you, I was an agent with the FBI. Collins was told that, and he's a truthful man. The fact is that I am with a government agency, but, as you guessed on that first day, that information has to be withheld because of ongoing investigations."

"The old national security gambit?"

"Gambit or truth, it doesn't really matter which you choose to believe; it's the only answer you'll get. The other part of what I told you is also true. I knew Shelly Martin, and I was in that photo that you saw."

"Then you have seen the photo?"

"Of course, I was there when it was taken."

"I mean, you saw the actual picture that Shelly placed in this desk."

Smith chose his words carefully. "Evidently, it has gone missing, so what would it matter if I saw it or not. I think that I have answered enough of your questions; I want to hear your theory on what happened."

"I think," said Davis, "that Shelly was killed," the word 'kill' shuddered through his lips, "she was killed, not because of what she knew, but because of who she knew. She knew all the people that passed through Elkhorn, and yet didn't."

"Now you're talking double-talk," interrupted Smith.

"No, I'm not!" protested Davis. "If you look at the curriculum vitae of any of those people, you will not find the Elkhorn Institute listed, and you will not find any gaps in their employment history. Yet, according to Shelly, they spent years living in the Bendy Ditch Estates."

"What do you think goes on at that place? Is it some clandestine, illegal operation or an Al-Qaeda training camp?"

"No," offered Davis, choosing his words carefully. "There is nothing there but the exchange of ideas. People who are there and make it through the course come out with very strong opinions about the way the world should be. In that regard, Elkhorn, Al-Qaeda, and any school have that in common. In the end, the students become like their teachers. If the teachers are militants, so are the graduates; if they are tolerant, well, likewise. I think militancy is easier to teach. Pump someone up with self-righteous anger and people are likely to die."

"So what are the Elkhorn people taught to think?"

"Where do I begin?" said McGowan. "A lot of innocent stuff, I suppose. For instance, people ought to be able to keep everything they own."

"That hardly seems radical."

"I suppose that depends on what you think is your own," countered Davis. "In my career we are told that if we give something to another person, it no longer belongs to us. We have to let it go. That's what we mean; at least, that's what I mean by giving. I pay my taxes, for example, and it's no longer my money; it's the government's money. If I don't like how they spend it, I get to try to vote the bums out. At Elkhorn, it never stops being their money. They take high salaries with golden parachutes. Then they make the argument that the high salary and benefits packages are necessary to keep the *best leaders*. Then they get each other appointed to each other's corporate boards and compensation committees. They tie compensation to profits, and box up bad assets to fake a good bottom line.

"What they turn out to be *best* at is taking what they want and holding on to what they take. They want value for their dollar, which indirectly means, that they see no public obligation to the larger society. Every once in a while they throw a fish to a high profile charity, but that's just a diversion. They don't want a government that looks at the balance between what they take, and what they are willing to part with."

"No welfare state."

"Yes, I think they'd like government to be too

poor to fund a safety net. Privatize welfare, privatize Social Security. Don't tempt the politicians into redistributing their wealth. After all, to them, it's still their money, and they've already redistributed everything into their own pockets."

"But the privatizing of Social Security failed!" interjected Smith.

"Did it? Social Security is in deep trouble if people choose to retire, and the Boomers will soon be lining up to do just that. If you eliminate the retirement savings of the middle class and loan the rest so much money that they can never repay, gosh, who will be able to afford to retire? It's true that there's been no governmental reform on Social Security, but a handful of people managed to raise everybody else's retirement age while they secured their own. After all, *there are two kinds of people in this world, those who can afford to retire and those who only think they can.*"

Smith sat up a little straighter at the quotation from Shelly Martin. "And you think people would believe that? That some high positioned powerbrokers would risk pulling down a national economy to keep other people poor?"

"People have been convinced of stranger things. Back in the eighteenth century," continued McGowan, "Jonathan Swift wrote a satirical essay called 'A Modest Proposal'. In it he suggested that the children of the poor in Ireland would cease to be a burden on their parents, and would actually benefit society if they were stewed and eaten. It was a preposterous solution, cannibalism and infanticide, but some took him and the idea as a serious strategy."

"But they'd say that they haven't done anything illegal or outlandish. They are merely capitalists protecting the free enterprise system."

"They aren't capitalists," countered Davis. "They like thinking that they are protecting the economic ideals that made America wealthy in the first place. They like thinking of Adam Smith as an economist and *The Wealth of Nations* as the Bible of their corporate morality. But, Adam Smith was a moral philosopher who knew about unintended consequences. In fact, the system works because of them. He proposed that the pursuit of gain, on the part of some, created positive unintended consequences for the working classes. The factories that made the industrialists rich would give good paying jobs to the poor. The society as a whole would grow stronger and more secure in a cycle of interdependency. But now the working classes own a lot of the businesses through their savings and retirement accounts. They don't own a big enough piece of anything to be in charge. They sign over their proxies and the managers have more power than the owners. It's changed the whole formula. The Elkhorn crowd has created a culture that reproduces itself like a computer virus. When the markets seemed to be doing well, they quietly privatized the companies and divisions that were making money and threw the garbage into boxes filled with the common stocks of the small investors. They fed off the investments of people too small to exercise oversight, and kept the government distracted from regulation by screaming 'foul' at any suggestion that their privacy should be invaded."

"So you think that the corporate and financial power brokers are in charge?"

"In charge? Not at all. Ever heard of Ganesha?" Smith shook his head. "Never mind," continued Davis. "I don't think anyone is in charge. Ideas that are set loose have a way of replicating and taking on a life of their own until the unforeseen circumstances knock them down for a while."

"But you think ideas killed Shelly?"

"She was killed because she knew the connections between a lot of people. If she spoke up with a credible voice, their empty boxes would start to stink." This statement by Davis should have made no sense at all, but Smith seemed to understand completely. The reaction convinced McGowan that he had mastered the vocabulary of Elkhorn.

"But you have no proof."

"You have the emails from my computer."

"Both your computer and Martin's were clean."

"I have a hard copy of a key email," argued Davis.

"Something typed on a piece of paper? Anyone could manufacture that. You need a time and date that relates it to a message server."

"Speaking of dating documents," began McGowan, "what kind of car are you driving?"

"Not a gray one with a vanity plate, if that's what you mean?" said the agent. "Let me tell you what we have so that you can measure the power of your conjecture in a court of law. We have a body. When the snow is cleared away, there will be a brass button at the scene. It will perfectly match one of the extra buttons that was sewn inside Ferguson's favorite sport coat. We found a telephone message taped on a digital recorder. The original came in on the office answering machine two weeks before Shelly disappeared. It is the same message that you heard played on Jerry's cell phone. The digital recorder is in a desk drawer in his house."

"That is crap!"

"And crap stinks. Anything can be made to look like anything."

"And I am supposed to watch a friend being destroyed by being dragged through a trial and imprisoned for the murder of a wife that he loved?"

"Not at all. Then I suppose that you have not heard the news."

"What?" asked Davis.

"There has been an accident on I-70 in Indiana. It appears that a snow plow ran your friend off the road. His car hit an abutment on an overpass. He died instantly. It probably was a tragic accident caused by the weather, but then again, he might have had such remorse over killing his wife that he intentionally drove into the blade. Anything can be made to look like anything."

"You bastard!"

"I am only telling you what I know, Dr. McGowan. We are both being very honest. You can make accusations, but they will not serve the memory of your friends. To counter your theory, those lined up against you would simply produce physical evidence to show that this is some sort of time-delayed murder/suicide."

"And, if I am quiet?"

"It looks to me like a double tragedy that fell on two people. We'll probably never know exactly what happened to Shelly, but there are so many reasons for violence today. Jerry, well, he probably was rushing home too fast when he heard the news that a body was found.

"What you have, Dr. McGowan, is a theory in search of evidence. In my business that is called 'nothing'. On the other hand, domestic violence is very common, and the spouse is usually mixed into the story. Things happen by accident, and then guilt kicks in. I can see someone like you hanging yourself on a bed sheet in prison when it finally hit you that you had killed your own wife. Her name is Beth, isn't it?"

He stood up and moved toward the door. "I can find my own way out. The weather is still bad out there; you may want to go home early to your wife."

Davis wanted to leave, but first he made a phone call. He was relieved when Beth answered.

"Everything okay, Honey?" he asked.

"You're the one who's driving in the snow," she countered, "I'm stuck here with cabin fever. They did plow the street, however, so nothing is slowing down much. Even the meter reader made it through."

"What?"

"They came inside to read the water meter, but I thought they had changed everything over to a remote monitoring system. I asked them that, and they said that they were verifying the accuracy of the new system."

"They?"

"Yes, there were two of them, a man and a woman. It only took them a minute, but I told them that they could have chosen better weather."

"That's true," said Davis, who was hoping that the anxiety in his chest was not leaking out through his lips. "I'm setting out for home. From what you said, the roads should be fine so it'll just be fifteen minutes. We'll just hunker down with popcorn and a movie for the evening. Is there anything you need me to pick up on the way home?"

"No, I think we're okay unless you had a movie in mind?"

"No, a nice predictable rerun off our shelf sounds good to me right now," said Davis. "Just stay put, okay?"

"Stay put? Where would I go?"

"You're right, Beth. I'll be home soon. I love you."

"I love you, too."

McGowan's hand was shaking as he returned the phone to its cradle. He was in over his head. Had Agent Abedinejad been threatening him at the very moment that strangers were in his house? He had the suspicion, however, that if he called the city, there would be someone there who would attest that the water department had crews out during a snowstorm to check the accuracy of the remote meter reading system.

One thing was certain, he had no evidence of anything. Anything that had been collected in the course of the so-called investigation had fallen into a black hole. Shelly had told him that Marlene Zeller's mother had died, and why would she have lied? Yet, someone showed up at Zeller's funeral playing the part.

His thoughts were interrupted by the phone's ring. He reached for it and answered, "St. Andrew's Church."

"Davis?" It was Beth, but her voice was nearly indistinguishable through her tears.

"What's wrong?" There was a silence, and McGowan could visualize her expression as she collected herself.

"Jerry is dead. The report just came over the news. He was killed in a weather-related accident on I-70."

It was Davis' turn to hold silence. "I'll be right home."

"Be careful."

How careful could he be?

Chapter Twenty-six

Endings

A memorial service was held at St. Andrew's the week before Christmas. The doors of the church were opened two hours before the service so that people could gather in an informal setting. The congregation of St. Andrew's had not really had much of a chance to know these two fine people, but their loss cast the future into uncertainty. Additionally, the event drew the media, and, to Davis' surprise, a bus load of passengers from two congregations in South Dakota. McGowan recognized Ronnie from the desk of the Bendy Ditch Hotel, but the young man never came anywhere close to him. Obviously, the townspeople had loved Shelly; most of them were here, even if the Institute people were not.

Grace was there on behalf of Jerry's family. For Shelly, there was no one. The decision had been made to cremate both bodies. In a symbolic gesture their ashes were mixed together and then divided so that half would be interred in the same graves with their previous partners. The people from Miller and the people from Elkhorn accepted responsibility for this last act of respect.

Davis had wanted to vilify the people from Elkhorn, but he couldn't. Their affection was too real. The people of St. Andrew's wanted a wall of photographs of Jerry and Shelly, but their house had been stripped of most of them. There were pictures, however, of the welcoming parties and home gatherings that had become the staple of the new pastors. Grace brought photos from her home. Pictures of Jerry growing up like the big brother that he was. In one he was wearing a cowboy hat, and that pleased the folk from the Dakotas. And there were pictures of Jerry's father. In one the two were in their pulpit robes. Grace said it was taken right after Jerry's ordination where his father was invited to preach.

"Does he know what happened?" asked Davis.

"I told him," said Grace, "but he keeps asking when Jerry is going to visit."

"If it's alright, I'd like to visit him some time. Our daughter lives nearby so it would be easy for us."

"That would be very kind," she said.

The people from Elkhorn also brought pictures, and McGowan had to push back his urge to try identifying Institute faces in the photos. "This is not evidence," he kept saying to himself, "this is the closest thing to justice that I can give. To have them remembered without taint or rancor."

The sound of the organ playing was the signal for the people to move out of the fellowship hall and into the sanctuary for the service. McGowan watched from the back as the room filled. In such services, the family would be last to be seated, and it was the responsibility of the minister to escort them to their seats at the front of the sanctuary. In this case, however, Grace Ferguson was alone. She walked alongside of Davis as the soprano soloist sang the aria, "I Know that my Redeemer Lives," from Handel's *Messiah*. When Grace reached the front pew, she was glad to see that Beth was waiting to sit beside her.

This was one of those times when McGowan was grateful for a prescribed order of service. As he read through the scriptures, he found himself taking on the consolation meant for the grieving. At the same time, however, he burned with the injustice of unanswered questions. Here were two people whose life together began in the common experience of faith and grief. In Davis' view of things, grief is the inevitable response to loss, and faith, the indomitable will to live with trust beyond all loss.

"The popular holiday songs tell us that home is the place to be during this time of year. Yet, you are all here, away from the shopping and preparations that mark the usual frenzy of these days. You're here because of two people who have given up a lot of

Christmases to be with you. Ministers are expected to be in church on Christmas Eve, so there's little opportunity for them and their families to pack up the car or get on a plane to travel to the place that they think of as home. This year, you have traveled to this place at a very busy time. I suspect it is because, in some part, Shelly and Jerry have become part of your family, just as you have become theirs.

"I can't pretend to understand what has happened in these last weeks. The events that led to this service are senseless and leave us with questions that may remain unanswered. The answer that is clear, however, is that Jerry and Shelly lived with a very clear sense of what they felt was important. They had the gift of being able to see all kinds of people as members of their family. They were always ready to place the real needs of their weakest neighbor ahead of their own, and they were willing to challenge the phoniness of race and class.

"Jerry's sister, Grace, is here. Of course, she is a member of the family, but so are we. Today we have gathered as a group of strangers, in order to grieve like a family. While we can honor the hope and faith that our sister and brother lived, we also share something else. We share a family resemblance. The traits of this family are not genetic, but they show up as shared values. Shelly and Jerry were people who could have become cynical. They had seen and experienced loss. Instead of becoming bitter, they chose to stand alongside the beds of the sick, and to move ahead in a quest for simple justice. They were not motivated by money or power. They only wanted to see a better world for their having been here."

At the end of the service the crowd lingered, and the people from three congregations mixed freely around the picture gallery. Ronnie sought out Davis.

"Dr. McGowan," he began.

"Hello, Ronnie," answered Davis. Wilkins was surprised by the use of his surname.

"I met you once."

"I remember," said Davis.

"I want to apologize for the way that I treated you, and that I said that I didn't know Rev. Shelly."

"You don't need to apologize. I understand that everything was complicated that day, but you should know that Shelly only had kind things to say about you and your family. And with your being here, that's the way I see it, too."

** ** **

Christmas Eve came so quickly on the heels of the funeral that it felt strange to be in the same room for such different reasons. On the other hand, there was life in the congregation that evening. Bessie

229

Hollows came down the church aisle pushing her walker. Trisha and Randy were having their youngest baptized. The one-year-old was a little old to play the baby Jesus in the pageant, but no one seemed to mind and she snuggled against Davis as he lifted her in his arms. They had put off the baptism until the new pastors arrived. Now, it seemed better to have grandma there and the minister who had been kind, like Shelly. That was the seven o'clock family service, but there was still the eleven o'clock candlelight service. McGowan was convinced that it would be difficult to mess up Christmas Eve. All it took was candles and carols and the people were lost in their own nostalgia. The people he was really thinking about were the ones who were not present, the ones who found no joy in the season of joy, no peace in a world of violence.

By a quarter past midnight the sanctuary had emptied, and Davis sat alone.

"Are you coming home?" called Beth from the back of the church.

"You go ahead," he answered, "I'll be along shortly. I have to get the lights." They had come in two cars.

"Merry Christmas, Love," she said.

"Merry Christmas, Beth."

In a few minutes he heard the door close, and knew that she had gone. He went into the sacristy and began throwing the breakers to turn off the main lighting. It was the dim light of the narthex that led him back toward the offices. There was a man standing in the vestibule. At first Davis thought it was an usher making sure the building was secured, and then he thought it might be a vagrant attracted to the lights. The man turned toward him. It was Agent Smith.

"Davis," he began. His voice was not confrontational. "I don't like the way this turned out."

"Agent Smith?"

"John," he said, "that part of my name is real."

He held out his hand. McGowan cautiously shook it.

"Davis, there's no surveillance here, so I will talk to you very plainly. Frankly, you deserve it. I lived in Elkhorn, and owe so much more to Shelly Martin than I can ever repay. I thought you should know that. The last time we talked you told me about Jonathan Swift. He also said, 'We have just enough religion to make us hate, but not enough to make us love one another.' Shelly taught me that.

"In my job, like yours, there are times when you are not supposed to feel. They tell us that feelings can blind you. They keep you from being able to tell the good guys from the bad. The truth is everyone I've ever met thinks they are the good guys and the other ones are bad. I think that you said this the other day, or maybe that's just what I took away from what you were telling me.

"Anyway, I have come to the conclusion that anyone who expects more from other people than they do from themselves is headed for trouble. People want to be rescued, but, otherwise, left alone. They want to take in what they think they deserve and hold on to what is theirs. I didn't see that in Shelly or Jerry or you. I've been on this assignment for years, and I have no idea where that elephant-headed deity is going to heave that tusk, but I hope more people start thinking more about others. This has turned out badly for innocent people, but I don't have to tell you that, do I?

"I think they'll leave you alone now. My prayer tonight was that the craziness stops soon. Peace."

"Peace would be very nice," thought McGowan, but John turned and was out the door before Davis could say anything. He stood at the glass enfolded entry for a long moment. He didn't know if he should expect an answer. None came.

Chapter Twenty-seven

Hello

Christmas Day was quiet around the McGowan house. Beth and Davis made phone calls to Bozeman, Montana and Indianapolis. The grandchildren spoke as long as they could hold their energy away from freshly opened packages. They would make the trip to Indiana on Sunday the twenty-sixth after Davis preached his final sermon at St. Andrew's.

The winter quarter would begin soon and McGowan had to get back to the syllabuses he had readied for his new classes. He would be glad to return to a campus crowded with people, where life followed a ten-week cycle and students presented problems of a different sort. The Presbytery had also kept its promise by limiting his time to six weeks. After the news broke of the two deaths, the executive had arranged for an interim pastor to help the congregation work through its shock and grief. The new person would be in the pulpit on the first Sunday of the New Year.

In the evening he called Jerry's sister, Grace, in

Indianapolis.

"Grace, this is Davis. We're going over your way for a few days after Christmas. If it's okay, I'd like to drop in on your father."

"That would be very kind of you Davis; I spent the day with him. Didn't seem much like Christmas. He thought I was my Mom."

"Does he talk about Jerry?"

"He's just in and out. When he's real quiet, I think he remembers, but then he's back in the past and talking to the nurses and aides like they are parishioners from one of his churches. They just go along with it. It keeps him from getting confused."

"Well, we will be driving near your exit on I-70, so we'll meet you on the way into the city."

** ** **

It was about two in the afternoon when he and Beth met Grace in the outer lobby of the extended care facility. They hugged all around. Davis could see her eyes welling up.

"How's he doing today?" he asked.

"He's fairly sharp and expecting company," she said. "I've explained who you are and it seems like he's retaining some of it. You caught him on a good day."

Grace led the McGowans back to the locked

hallway that kept the dementia patients corralled in one area. As they moved toward the nurses' station at the center of the pod, a small man struggled to rise on his spindly legs.

"That's Dad," whispered Grace. "You can tell he's excited."

"It is so good that you came," he called out "I knew you would come. Didn't I tell you, Gracie, that he would come today? After all, it's Christmas."

"Dad, Christmas was yesterday, remember?"

"That's all right," said Davis. "Maybe it's his Christmas."

The frail man turned to Beth, "Don't tell me, Jerry, this must be your new bride. I get forgetful sometimes, and I can't remember your name, Dear."

"Shelly," said Beth, "it's nice to see you."

"That's right, Shelly, I remember now. Did I know how pretty you are?"

"I think this is the first time she's been able to visit, Dad," said Grace.

He turned to McGowan and latched hold of his arm. "Oh, Jerry, I've really been missing you, Son. I thought that you might never come back."

"It's good to be home, Dad."

Acknowledgements and Disclaimer

Writers spend a good deal of time in isolation. When we emerge from the fog of our imaginations we rely on readers to provide perspective on the story. In the case of *McGowan's Retreat*, I owe a debt of gratitude to Chuck Duffy, Jean-Luc and Denise Lo Cicéro, Larry Smith, and the Firelands Writer's Group. By sheer coincidence, and like Davis McGowan, my son lives in Bozeman, Montana. I need to thank Court Smith for introducing me to the phrase "Cowboy up." As ever, Nancy Brady Smith read and reread the manuscript until she knew it better than I. This book is dedicated to her.

Like me, Davis McGowan teaches at Wright State University. Unlike me, however, his tenure, students, and colleagues are purely fictional.

Rob Smith

Rob Smith
resides on Ohio's
north coast where he
writes and works to
restore a thirty year old British sloop.
He holds a bachelor's degree from
Westminster College in Pennsylvania
and master and doctoral degrees from
Princeton Theological Seminary.

Davis McGowan made his first appearance in *McGowan's Call* which was pub-
lished in 2007.

Drinian Press/

Enquiry Series

The Enquiry Series presents books that explore the boundaries between literature and culture. The series began with *Hogwarts, Narnia, and Middle Earth*, an inquiry into the biblical themes in the work of three authors of popular fiction. Most recently, Drinian Press has partnered with anthropologists engaged in cross-cultural projects. While The Enquiry Series provides educational resources which are outside our primary focus on book-length fiction, they underscore the direct link between literature and community formation.

Our World, Our Stories
Edited by
Wm Dustin Cantrell and Elizabeth J. Pfeiffer
978-0978516581   80 pages
(color Illustrated)

Cultural Perspectives on the Bible
by Rob Smith
978-0978516574   244 pages

Hogwarts, Narnia, and Middle Earth
by Rob Smith
978-0978516567   124 pages

www.DrinianPress.com

Breinigsville, PA USA
20 August 2009
222528BV00003B/7/P